"I can't stop thi... kiss we shared i... you... told her.

"It was just a kiss."

"A kiss that keeps me awake at night and haunts my dreams."

"A kiss that never should have happened," Ashley said firmly, refusing to admit that the memory of that moment had the exact same effect on her.

"We were always good together, Ash."

She swallowed. "Were—past tense."

"That kiss proves nothing is finished between us."

Dear Reader,

Every woman remembers her first love—and her first heartbreak. Cameron Turcotte was both for Ashley Roarke, and when he left town she was sure she'd never love anyone as much as she'd loved him.

Of course, a lot can change in twelve years, and when Cam comes back after that time, Ashley has no intention of picking up where they left off.

But Cam knows the one thing that hasn't changed is the chemistry between him and Ashley—if only he can convince her that first love sometimes deserves a second chance.

I hope you enjoy their story.

All the best,

Brenda Harlen

THE
PREGNANCY
PLAN

BRENDA HARLEN

Silhouette®

SPECIAL EDITION®

Published by Silhouette Books

America's Publisher of Contemporary Romance

SILHOUETTE BOOKS

ISBN-13: 978-0-373-65520-5

THE PREGNANCY PLAN

Copyright © 2010 by Brenda Harlen

Recycling programs
for this product may
not exist in your area.

This is a work of fiction. Names, characters, places and incidents are
either the product of the author's imagination or are used fictitiously, and
any resemblance to actual persons, living or dead, business establishments,
events or locales is entirely coincidental.

This edition published by arrangement with Harlequin Books S.A.

For questions and comments about the quality of this book please contact us
at Customer_eCare@Harlequin.ca.

® and TM are trademarks of Harlequin Books S.A., used under license.
Trademarks indicated with ® are registered in the United States Patent
and Trademark Office, the Canadian Trade Marks Office and in other
countries.

Visit Silhouette Books at www.eHarlequin.com

Printed in U.S.A.

BRENDA HARLEN

grew up in a small town surrounded by books and imaginary friends. Although she always dreamed of being a writer, she chose to follow a more traditional career path first. After two years of practicing as an attorney (including an appearance in front of the Supreme Court of Canada), she gave up her "real" job to be a mom and to try her hand at writing books. Three years, five manuscripts and another baby later, she sold her first book—an RWA Golden Heart winner—to Silhouette Books.

Brenda lives in southern Ontario with her real-life husband/hero, two heroes-in-training and two neurotic dogs. She is still surrounded by books ("too many books," according to her children) and imaginary friends, but she also enjoys communicating with "real" people. Readers can contact Brenda by e-mail at brendaharlen@yahoo.com or by snail mail c/o Silhouette Books, 233 Broadway, Suite 1001, New York, NY 10279.

To Shelly and Brett

High school sweethearts who,
twenty-three years later, are still going strong.

Thanks for the example and the inspiration.

Chapter One

"**I**'m going to have a baby."

Ashley Roarke's statement, made to her sister and her cousin over Sunday brunch, was met by silence.

She glanced from Megan to Paige and back again, but she couldn't tell what either of them was thinking.

Paige Wilder, a family law attorney who was accustomed to responding quickly to unexpected revelations in court, recovered first. "You're pregnant?"

"Not yet."

Megan Richmond, a research scientist, took a moment to absorb the news and consider before she said, "I didn't even know you were dating anyone."

Ashley swirled a piece of French toast in the maple syrup on her plate, focusing all of her attention on the task. "I'm not."

"Then you're going to have to explain this to me," her sister—recently and very happily married—said.

Ashley nibbled on the sweet bread while she considered her response.

Megan and Paige weren't just family, they were her best friends, and she'd always been able to count on their unequivocal support in whatever she chose to do. Though she wasn't sure they would support her in this, she also wouldn't be dissuaded.

"I made an appointment at PARC," she finally said, using the acronym for the Pinehurst Assisted Reproduction Clinic.

Megan set her cup down and turned to Paige. "This is all your fault."

"What did I do?"

"You were the one who insisted she didn't need a husband to have a baby."

"Well, she doesn't. And she certainly doesn't need a husband like CBB," her cousin said, invoking the nickname she'd bestowed upon Ashley's ex-fiancé.

His real name was Trevor, but after the breakup of their engagement, he'd been referred to as Cheating Bastard Byden, and the initials had stuck.

It was Paige who'd discovered that Trevor was cheating. She'd seen him cozied up in a booth at a restaurant with a colleague, and while she didn't want to believe he would be unfaithful to his fiancée, the evidence had been irrefutable. Ashley knew that Paige hated telling her, but she would have hated even more for the deception to continue.

Of course, Ashley had refused to believe her. She'd even— she was embarrassed to admit now—accused Paige of being jealous of her happiness. In fact, she'd been so positive that her cousin was wrong, she'd gone straight to Trevor.

She'd expected him to reassure her of his love and fidelity. And while he did insist that he loved her, and that he'd never felt about anyone else the way he felt about her, he'd also admitted that he'd been with other women.

Not another woman—singular, but other women—plural.

And Ashley had felt as if the ground had crumbled beneath her feet.

He'd tried to explain that he'd been feeling a little uncertain since their engagement, and that every woman he'd been with since had reassured him that he was marrying the only woman he would ever love, and he promised her that he would never even look at another woman after they were married.

Ashley was not reassured. As far as she was concerned, he'd made a vow when he'd asked her to marry him, and if he couldn't honor that vow before the wedding, she knew nothing would change afterward.

She didn't regret ending their relationship, but she'd been looking forward to her wedding day since she was a little girl. As she'd grown older, her dreams had taken on a more specific focus. It wasn't just that she wanted a wedding, she wanted to be married. She wanted to fall in love and build a future— and a family—with a man who loved her, too.

She'd thought Trevor was that man. And when she'd handed back his ring, she'd relinquished some of her dreams, too.

That had been almost four months ago. Since then, she'd given the matter a lot of thought. The more she thought about it, the more she resented having to put her life on hold because she'd been wrong about Trevor.

And she'd decided she wasn't going to put her life on hold any longer.

"You can't blame Paige for this," Ashley told her sister now. "I would have thought about artificial insemination on my own if I hadn't been so preoccupied with planning my wedding."

Paige wrinkled her nose. "Anything 'artificial' can't be very much fun."

"I'm not doing it for fun. I'm doing it to have a baby."

"Just because CBB turned out to be a first-class CB doesn't

mean you should give up hope of finding a wonderful man to father your children," Megan said.

"I haven't given up," Ashley denied, though she wasn't entirely sure it was true. Two broken hearts in one lifetime were too many for her. "But I'm tired of waiting."

"You're not even thirty yet," Paige reminded her.

"But I'm no closer to having a husband and a baby than I was at twenty," she pointed out to both of them. "I was devastated when I found out that Trevor was cheating on me. But I'm not sure if I was really heartbroken by his betrayal or because he derailed my hopes of having a child. And I began to wonder if one of the reasons I accepted Trevor's proposal in the first place was that he seemed to want marriage and a family as much as I do."

"That doesn't excuse what he did," Paige said fiercely.

"No, it doesn't," Ashley agreed. "But it made me realize that I want a baby more than I want a husband."

"But your engagement only ended four months ago," Megan said gently. "You have to give your heart time to heal."

"How much time?" Ashley wanted to know. "How long am I supposed to wait until you'll trust that I've considered all the angles, that this is what I really want to do?"

"More than four months," her sister told her.

"We know how much you want a child of your own," Paige chimed in. "And how much love you have to give. But I think we're both concerned that this is an impulse, an emotional response to the breakup of your engagement."

"I'm going to have a baby, and nothing either of you say is going to change my mind now," Ashley assured her.

"I don't want to change your mind," Paige said. "I just want you to rethink your options."

"The Pinehurst clinic has a reputation for excellence and a record of success."

"I know it does," her cousin admitted. "But did you know that Cameron Turcotte is back in town?"

Her cousin's question seemed to come from out of the blue, but Ashley knew the remark wasn't unintentional. Because even after twelve years, just the mention of his name was enough to make her heart skip a beat, but she wouldn't—couldn't—let Paige know it.

"Who?" she said instead.

"I know you saw him at the reunion," Paige said, referring to the high school reunion they'd all attended a few months earlier. Although Cam had been two years ahead of Ashley in school, the party had been open to all former graduates in celebration of Hill Park High School's one hundredth year anniversary.

She shrugged. "So we talked."

"And maybe your…talk…had something to do with his decision to come back to Pinehurst."

Megan frowned, and Ashley knew her sister had concerns about Cameron's return—specifically how it would affect Ashley.

"Is it true, then, that he's going to be working with Elijah Alexander?" Megan asked.

Paige nodded.

"So Cam's back," Ashley said. "So what? What does that have to do with anything?"

"It just seems to me that someone who spent so many years in medical school would have a pretty good idea about how to make a baby," Paige teased.

Ashley didn't doubt that it was true, but she had no intention of letting her mind wander down that dead-end path.

Cameron Turcotte had been her first love, her first lover, and even way back when they were both in high school, he'd been a creative and considerate partner. He'd also broken her heart, and she wasn't going to forget that for a few horizontal thrills. Not even if he'd given her any indication that he was interested in a reunion of that kind, which he hadn't.

"You seem to be forgetting that one of the reasons Cam and I split up was that I wanted to have kids and he didn't."

"He didn't want a baby twelve years ago," Paige pointed out. "I wouldn't be surprised if he's changed his mind since then."

"Well, I've changed mine, too," Ashley said. "I'm no longer looking for a marriage proposal or even a relationship. All I want is a sperm donor."

"You're really not interested?" Megan asked skeptically.

"I'm really not interested."

But while Ashley's voice rang with conviction, her heart wasn't quite so certain.

When Cameron Turcotte first contacted the real estate company, it was to inquire about available rental properties in the area. Since he wasn't convinced that the move back to Pinehurst would be a permanent one, it seemed logical to rent rather than buy. But he didn't want an apartment; he wanted a house, a place to go at the end of the day that was his alone without neighbors above and below him. Unfortunately, house rentals were apparently rare in the area and Tina Stilwell hadn't sounded optimistic about his prospects.

But she'd called earlier in the day to let him know that the owners of a house she had listed might be willing to consider a one-year lease in the hopes that the housing market would pick up within that time and ultimately result in a higher sale price for the home.

Since Cam had committed to a one-year contract with Elijah Alexander—a trial period for both of them, with the possibility of buying into the practice at the end of that term if it was what they wanted—he figured a housing lease for the same amount of time would be ideal. So it was that after a ten-hour day, he wasn't heading back to his parents' retirement community bungalow, where he'd temporarily taken up residence, but following a much too perky real estate agent through the front door of a gorgeous stone and brick two-story.

"It's a wonderful neighborhood, close to the local schools and parks, convenient to shopping, entertainment, and pretty much anything else you'd want," she told him.

And only a short drive from Dr. Alexander's offices, he'd noted.

"I can walk through with you, if you want," Tina said, as she led him from the living room through the dining room to the kitchen at the back of the house, from plush carpet to glossy hardwood to cool travertine. "But I find a lot of clients prefer to look around on their own."

"I'll wander, and let you know if I have any questions," he said, accepting the spec sheet she'd taken from the upright display on the long granite counter in the kitchen.

The agent nodded, pulling out her BlackBerry as she settled at one of the high-backed stools lined up by the breakfast bar.

He exited the kitchen through another doorway, passing a family room and den as he made his way toward the stairs. On the upper level he found four bedrooms, all of them generously sized with lots of windows to ensure plenty of natural light.

The master bedroom at the back of the house was enormous—or maybe it just seemed so because it was devoid of furniture, as were all the other rooms in the house—with a huge walk-in closet and a four-piece ensuite bath of gleaming marble and glistening chrome. Returning to the main part of the room, he wandered over to the pair of wide windows overlooking a professionally landscaped backyard complete with a stone patio, pond, and decorative beds filled with colorful blooms and greenery.

Best of all, there was still a lot of open space, enough room for a child to run around. Several children even, he thought, and sighed with regret that his marriage hadn't worked out quite the way he'd planned.

When he'd proposed to Danica Carrington, he'd known that she was focused on her career to the exclusion of all else; she'd made no secret of the fact that children weren't part of her plan. He'd married her anyway, certain that she would change her mind when she held their baby in her arms. But it hadn't happened that way at all, and after three years of desperately trying to make their marriage work, he'd finally given up and she'd eagerly walked away.

He pushed aside the disappointments and continued his tour. There was no reason to think of Danica now, to continue to mourn what had never been anything more than an illusion. He was determined to put the past behind him and make a fresh start in Pinehurst, to make a new life with Madeline.

And one of the most attractive features of this home, from his point of view, was its move-in condition. The walls were freshly painted in neutral colors, the carpets were pristine, the hardwood unmarked and the cherry kitchen was a chef's paradise.

Not that he was a chef, by any stretch of the imagination, but he enjoyed experimenting in the kitchen. And he knew he would enjoy experimenting in that kitchen, with its top-of-the-line stainless steel appliances, luxurious island and two sets of French doors opening onto a cedar deck.

Tina tucked her BlackBerry away when he paused at those doors to survey the backyard more closely.

"Any thoughts?" she asked him.

I want it, was the first thought that came to mind.

"It's probably a lot more space than I need," he said instead.

"It is spacious," she agreed, choosing to put a positive spin on his negative comment. "More suited to a family than a single man, but definitely a good investment."

"It's certainly been immaculately maintained."

"It's a three-year-old custom-design by Armstrong & Sullivan, built by Carson Construction," she said. "The owners are both young professionals who, from what I understand, spent more time at their jobs than at home."

He knew what that kind of life was like—and the toll it could take on a marriage. But all he said was, "Either they've taken minimalist decorating to a new level or they've already moved out."

"Moved out," she admitted, with a smile. "The wife got transferred to New York City, the husband took a job offer in Los Angeles, and they left me in charge of the house."

And Cam would bet the proceeds were to be split down the middle, along with all their other shared possessions, with a significant chunk from each side going to their respective bloodsucking lawyers.

Yeah, he'd been there, done that, too.

Of course, when he'd met Danica he'd thought she was the type of woman he wanted, someone who had ambitions and dreams, who wanted more than to be a wife and a mother.

Someone who didn't remind him of Ashley Roarke.

Since he'd been back in Pinehurst, it seemed as if everything reminded him of Ashley. Every street and shop and landmark brought back memories of times they'd spent together.

When he'd left town more than a dozen years ago, he'd left his high school sweetheart behind. He could have chosen a college closer to home and had, in fact, been far more tempted to do just that. Instead, he'd opted to put some serious distance between them, so that he wouldn't be able to come home on a long weekend, so that he wouldn't end up sacrificing his own dreams just because he was in love.

During his first few years away, he'd dated only occasionally, and the girls he had dated were usually blue-eyed blondes who reminded him of Ashley in some way. Not surprisingly, none of those relationships ever went very far.

An initial attraction sparked by a superficial resemblance to the girl he'd left behind inevitably fizzled when he finally accepted that no one else was Ashley. No one else's eyes were as bright, no one else's smile was so warm, no one else's touch felt so right.

And then he met a dark-haired, dark-eyed first-year law student who didn't resemble Ashley in any way.

Danica wasn't looking to get married; she didn't want to tie herself down. She had plans for her life and she wasn't going to let anything—or anyone—stand in the way of fulfilling them.

She was, it had seemed to him then, his perfect match.

It had taken him a long time to realize what a mistake he'd made.

He sometimes wondered how differently his life might have turned out if he'd never gone away. If he'd never said goodbye to Ashley. But wondering and wishing couldn't change the past, and though there had been more bumps in the road than he'd have chosen, he couldn't regret where he was now.

Now he had Madeline, and she was the reason for everything he did, for everything he was. She would probably expect him to consult with her before making a decision on their housing situation since it would impact her future, too. But she wouldn't be back from London for three more weeks and he didn't want to wait that long.

He needed to move into a place of his own. He loved his parents dearly—in fact, being closer to them was one of the reasons he'd decided to move out of Seattle and look for a job in the area. But he was too old to be sleeping on living room furniture, and he certainly couldn't share the couch with Madeline.

He considered calling her now, not just to tell her about the house but to hear her voice. But with the five-hour time difference, it was likely that she was already in bed.

He glanced at the spec sheet he still had in hand, then up at Tina. "What are they asking for rent?"

She told him the amount. "Plus utilities," she said, sounding apologetic.

"It would almost be cheaper to buy it," he noted.

"I think that's the point. They are willing to rent, but they'd rather sell."

Cam hesitated. He hadn't considered buying a house. On the other hand, real estate was generally a good investment and he had no doubt his mortgage payments would be less than the quoted rental fee.

"I know you were adamant about wanting a house," she said. "But I did find a couple of condos available for rent, and I've got the details with me if you want to take a look at those instead."

He wasn't usually impulsive, but something about this house just felt right. As if he and Madeline belonged there.

As if they'd finally come home.

And if it crossed his mind that being back in Pinehurst meant being near Ashley Roarke again, well, he pushed that thought aside.

Chapter Two

Ashley was a big fan of retail therapy. A great pair of shoes could put a smile on her face on the gloomiest of days, and she was positively beaming when she pulled onto Chetwood Street heading home after her shopping expedition Thursday afternoon.

Only two and a half weeks until the first day of school, and she was as excited as any of the first graders who would be entering her class.

She'd enjoyed the summer break and had, in fact, needed both the time away from the classroom and the solitude to let her bruised and battered heart heal. But six weeks of intense rest and relaxation along with some quality time spent with Marg & Rita had her feeling a lot better about herself and her future. Okay, so maybe she'd wallowed a little, but she'd eventually pulled herself out of the funk and now she wasn't just ready but eager to move forward. Deciding to have a baby was a big step forward, but one she was more than ready to take.

Her already high spirits got another lift when she spotted the SOLD sign down the street. She hadn't known the previous owners except to say hello in passing, but she'd heard that they were newlyweds when they'd first moved in and now, three years later, newly divorced. Maybe that was part of the reason she'd felt inexplicably saddened when they'd packed up, or maybe she'd just hated to think that the beautiful home had been abandoned, but today, the SOLD sign seemed to her another beacon of hope.

She pulled into her driveway already speculating about the new owners, wondering where they were from and when they'd move in. Were they another newlywed couple? Empty nesters? A family with kids? The neighborhood was an eclectic collection of each, including a few singles like herself.

Because she was thinking about her potential neighbors, she didn't see the package propped up against the door until she was sliding her key into the lock. It was wrapped in brown paper and blended in with the paint, suggesting that she really should repaint the door to give the outside a little boost of color and a more welcoming feel. Since she wasn't getting married and moving any time in the near future, she should consider adding some personal touches to make the house more distinctly her own.

She felt a slight pang when she thought of the wedding that wouldn't be, but only slight. She was totally over Trevor now and determined not to let the absence of a husband prevent her from having the child she wanted.

She shifted her other bags, then tucked the flat parcel under her arm and carried it inside. She dumped everything on top of the dining room table before backtracking to the kitchen.

She opened the fridge, found a can of her diet soda next to the regular Pepsi her sister favored and popped the top.

Megan had been married for three months now, but Ashley still missed having her around. She certainly missed her more than she missed her former fiancé—she shook her head, pushing him firmly out of her mind. She wasn't going to ruin a perfectly nice day thinking about Trevor and what he'd done.

Instead, she carried her drink into the dining room, back to the mysterious paper-wrapped package. She couldn't remember buying anything that needed to be delivered, but the neatly printed label had her name and address on it, so she turned the parcel over and lifted the tape.

As she pulled back the paper, revealing a polished walnut frame and the edge of a cream-colored mat, she realized it was a picture. Tearing the paper further, she sucked in a breath at the image of herself wrapped in the arms of her supposedly devoted fiancé.

The frame slipped from her fingers and crashed to the ground.

The glass broke, a long jagged crack across the center, slicing neatly between the images of Ashley and Trevor.

She'd canceled the wedding and everything related to it. She'd made the phone calls herself to the florist and the caterer; she'd notified the band and the pastry chef. She'd been too late to stop the order at the printer, but she'd been certain to shred each and every invitation and response card and personalized thank-you note when they were delivered. She knew there was no way she would have forgotten to contact the photographer.

Then she spotted the piece of paper tucked into the bottom corner of the frame. She reached for it, frowning as she unfolded it. If it was an invoice—

No, it was a note.

From Trevor.

Ashley,

I just wanted you to know that I've been thinking about you and missing you. I haven't given up hope that we can find a way to work things out. I'm sending this picture to remind you of the happy times we had together, and to let you know that I want us to be together again.

I love you.

T xo

She tore the note into tiny pieces and let them fall from her hands like confetti. Of course, thinking of confetti made her think of weddings and that made her even angrier.

She picked up the broken frame and carted it to the kitchen to dump it in the garbage where it belonged. She was over him. She really was. Wholly and completely. But apparently she wasn't over being mad.

She pulled the waste basket out of the cupboard and shoved the picture in it, determined to put Trevor out of her mind. As she pushed down on it, she felt a quick, slicing pain. She felt the blood, warm and wet, dripping down her hand, before she saw the streaks of red. And when she did, her stomach pitched.

She'd never done well with the sight of blood. Although cuts and scrapes were common occurrences with first graders, those cuts and scrapes could usually be fixed with a Band-Aid or an ice pack. Ashley peeked at her hand again and didn't think a Band-Aid was going to do the job. Not this time.

She grabbed a clean dish towel from the drawer and wrapped it around her palm.

A quick glance at the clock revealed that it was almost five, so she knew that the phones at her doctor's office would already have been turned over to the answering service. But she'd been a patient of Uncle Eli's since she was a child and the duration of their relationship, combined with the fact that he'd been a good friend of both of her parents, meant that she could show up at his office at this late hour and know that he would make time for her. Hopefully that would save her a trip to the emergency room.

Fifteen minutes later, she was ushered into an exam room by the nurse.

"The doctor will be in to see you shortly," Irene told her.

And Ashley, feeling a little queasy from the loss of blood, nodded gratefully, reassured that she'd made the right decision in coming here rather than the hospital.

An opinion that changed as soon as the doctor walked into the room.

Cam had been at the office since 8:00 a.m.

He knew that the nature of a family practice required a certain degree of flexibility with respect to unexpected emergencies, but as the day wore on and he worked through lunch, he wished that Courtney—the receptionist and general office manager—would show some appreciation of the same fact and schedule appointments with more than ten minutes between them.

By five o'clock, the number of patients in the waiting room had diminished sufficiently that there were enough chairs for those still waiting. By that same time, he'd managed to take half a dozen bites of the sandwich that Courtney had brought back for him when she returned from her lunch break. The thinning of the crowd combined with the silencing of his stomach gave him hope that he might actually get out of the office before he needed to return the following morning.

He was reaching for the file in the slot outside of exam room number two when Irene—Dr. Alexander's sister and longtime nurse—slipped out of room number four. The guilty flush in her cheeks warned him that she'd squeezed in yet another patient who didn't have an appointment.

He sighed. "I thought you wanted to go home as much as I do."

"You need a home in order to go to it," she said.

"I'll have one soon enough," he told her. "And you're not going to distract me that easily."

"I'm not trying to distract you at all." She took his arm and steered him towards the door she'd just exited.

"I thought Mrs. Kirkland was next."

"Mrs. Kirkland is a hypochondriac, but this patient is really bleeding."

He sighed again and took the folder she thrust into his hands, not even having a moment to note the name on the tab before he walked in the room.

And found himself face-to-face with Ashley Roarke.

He faltered, at a sudden loss for words since "Hello, Ashley, I'm Dr. Turcotte"—the standard greeting he'd given to Dr. Alexander's other patients—seemed a little ridiculous in light of their history.

But it was long ago history and he'd seen her only once since he'd left town more than a dozen years earlier—just a few months before at their high school reunion. Ashley had made it clear to him then then that she didn't forgive him for leaving her and that she had no interest in reminiscing with him.

She'd also told him that she was getting married in a few months, he remembered now. But her purse was clutched in her left hand and the impressive diamond she'd worn at the reunion wasn't on it.

Her other hand was wrapped in a bloody towel, and it was the blood that jerked him out of the past and firmly back into doctor mode.

He couldn't think of her as the first woman he'd ever

loved, the only woman he'd never forgotten. She was a patient, and it was his job to ascertain the nature of her injury and prescribe treatment.

"I, uh, came to see Eli," she told him, breaking the awkward silence.

"He's at the hospital."

"Oh. Well." She cleared her throat. "Okay. I'll go there then. To the hospital. To catch up with him there."

She was babbling, obviously not any more prepared for this unexpected meeting than he was. And though he was tempted to let her go, it was apparent that she hadn't come to chat with Eli but for medical attention, and he wouldn't shirk his duty.

"You're dripping blood," he told her.

She glanced down, and quickly averted her gaze again.

"I think I should take a look at that before you go anywhere." He reached into a box on the counter to pull out a pair of disposable gloves.

"I'd rather have Eli look at it," she said.

"Stop being stubborn, Ash."

"I'm not being stubborn," she denied. "I'd just feel more comfortable seeing my doctor."

Despite her close relationship with Elijah Alexander, she obviously hadn't heard that he wasn't doing patient rounds at the hospital but spending time with his wife, who was in ICU after suffering a near-fatal heart attack the previous evening.

So all he said to her was, "And I'd let you go if I didn't think it was likely you'd pass out while you were driving and potentially cause more harm to yourself and/or others."

He wouldn't have thought it was possible, but her face got even whiter. "Have I lost that much blood?"

He chuckled as he tugged on the second glove. "Hardly."

She scowled. "Then why do you think I'd pass out?"

"Because I was there when you fell off the stone wall at Eagle Point Park and cut your knee open. You said you were okay, then you saw the blood and your face went white just before your eyes rolled back in your head."

He shouldn't have mentioned the incident, because it was an admission that he still remembered that day, even so many years later. As he remembered so many things they'd done and moments they'd spent together. He had too many memories of Ashley. Memories that haunted his waking moments and taunted him in dreams.

"I was nine," she said, her indignant response forcing his attention back to the present.

"And you're as pale now as you were then," he told her.

Since she couldn't see her face, she really wasn't in a position to deny his accusation. Instead, she lifted her arm and thrust her towel-wrapped hand toward him.

"Fine. Take a look and give me one of those butterfly bandage things so I can go home."

Cam took her hand and carefully began unwrapping the towel. At another time, he might have lifted his brows at the parade of little goslings embroidered along the hem, but now it was the blood soaked into the fabric that held his attention.

"How did it happen?" he asked.

"Broken glass."

He was a doctor—he'd seen far worse than a three-inch gash in the flesh of a woman's hand. Except that this was Ashley's hand, and the gash ran down the side of her palm before abruptly detouring toward her wrist. Luckily, it stopped short of her ulnar artery, but his heart skipped a beat in his chest when he realized how close it had come.

"Must have been a big piece of glass," he noted.

"Eleven-by-fourteen."

It only took him a second to figure out the reference. "A picture frame."

She nodded, but kept her gaze firmly affixed to the opposite wall.

He tore open the packaging of a gauze pad, dabbed gently at the skin around the wound. "Well, I think it's going to take a little bit more than one of those butterfly bandage things to fix this up."

"How much more?"

"Probably ten to fifteen stitches."

He thought of the patients still in the waiting room and considered sending her to the hospital for the procedure. Now that he'd examined her injury, he was confident the repair was something any ER doctor could handle.

But she was already here and he had everything he needed on the premises to get the job done, and he would take care to minimize, as much as possible, any scarring.

"I was afraid you were going to say something like that." She sighed. "Okay. Let's just do it."

"Well, Ashley Roarke, I never thought I'd hear you say those words to me again," he teased.

That remark brought color to her too-pale cheeks and a flash to her lovely violet eyes.

Eyes that had haunted his thoughts and his dreams for longer than he was willing to admit.

"The stitches, *doctor.*"

He grinned, unrepentant. "Of course."

He released her hand and went to the door, poking his head out to ask Irene for a suture tray.

She must have anticipated his request, because she came in with the necessary equipment less than a minute later.

Her eyes grew wide when she saw Ashley's injury.

"Oh, honey, what have you done?"

"I lost a fight with a piece of broken glass," Ashley told her.

"Well, don't you worry. The doctor will have you fixed up in no time."

"But you're going to jab me with that first, aren't you?" she asked, warily eyeing the needle that the nurse was prepping.

"Actually, the doctor is going to jab you with it," Irene told her. "But you won't feel him poking at you after that."

Cam fought against a smile as Ashley's cheeks colored again.

He'd remembered so many things about her, but he'd forgotten how easily she blushed, how much he used to enjoy making her blush. But that was a long time ago.

Now he had to forget that they were ever lovers and concentrate on doing his job.

"There now. That wasn't so bad, was it?" Irene said.

"You wouldn't be asking that question if you'd been on the other end of the needle," Ashley told her.

The nurse chuckled. "You never did like getting shots," she remembered. "And your sister wasn't any better. How's she doing, by the way?"

He didn't know if Irene had asked the question because she was anxious to catch up on Roarke family gossip or if she was trying to distract Ashley from what he was doing, but since the patient wasn't paying any attention to him or the needle sliding through her skin, he was grateful.

"Meg's great," Ashley responded. "She seems to have adapted to marriage easily and blissfully."

"Good for her," the nurse asserted. Then her voice gentled when she said, "But I imagine it must have been difficult for you."

Ashley didn't move, but Cam sensed her tension.

"Megan getting married so soon after you ended your engagement, I mean," Irene clarified.

"I was—*am*—happy for her."

"Well, of course you are. And I have no doubt that someday you'll find a man who's perfect for you, too."

"I'm not looking for a man—perfect or otherwise," Ashley said.

She spoke with such conviction, he found himself wondering about the details of her broken engagement, and whether he might be able to subtly pry them out of the nurse at another time. Because he had no doubt that if there were details to be known, Irene would know them.

But for now, he clenched his teeth together to hold back the questions he wanted to ask. He had no business asking any questions, no business feeling anything for the woman who had once meant everything to him.

"Are you up to date with your tetanus shot?" he asked instead.

Ashley shifted her attention from the nurse to him. "I had a booster two years ago."

"Then you don't need another one."

"Must be my lucky day."

He smiled, appreciating that she could find humor in the situation.

"Since you're just about finished up here, I'll go check on Mrs. Kirkland," Irene told him. Then to Ashley, "Take care of yourself, hon."

"I will."

"How do they look?" he asked, after Irene had gone.

Ashley glanced down at her hand, at the dark thread that stood out in stark contrast to her pink skin. "It looks…good?"

He smiled again. "It looks raw and ugly, but it will look good when the wound has healed."

"How long?" she asked.

He tore open a sterile gauze pad, affixed it to her skin. "Seven to ten days."

"At least they'll be out before I go back to school."

"Too bad," he said. "I imagine fifteen stitches could be the object of intense fascination for a bunch of first graders."

She looked up, surprise evident in those stunning eyes.

He was suddenly aware of how close they were sitting. That he was still holding her hand. And that she had made no effort to pull away.

"How did you know I teach first grade?"

He shrugged. "It's what you always said you were going to do."

"I didn't think you would have remembered something like that," she murmured.

"You'd be surprised what I remember," he said. "What I couldn't forget."

Her gaze dropped away, and he cursed himself for speaking aloud a truth he'd only recently acknowledged.

He wrote her a prescription for some painkillers, tore off the page and handed it to her.

"Try to keep your hand elevated as much as possible, keep the stitches dry, and set up an appointment with Courtney to have them checked next week."

"I'll do that," she said. "Thanks."

Cam nodded and moved to the door, pausing with his hand on the knob.

"I never forgot you, Ashley. And I don't think you forgot me, either."

He walked out before she could reply. Because even if she denied it, even if she *had* forgotten about him, he was going to make sure she remembered him now.

This time, he wasn't going to walk away.

Chapter Three

Ashley didn't get the prescription filled.

She hadn't told Cam that she was taking Fedentropin because she didn't want him asking all kinds of questions about the drug trial she was participating in. It had been awkward enough when Irene had made reference to her broken engagement without getting into any explanations about her medical history or the experimental drug that was helping to manage her endometriosis so that pregnancy remained an option for her.

But her hand throbbed painfully as she tried to sweep up remnants of broken glass and wood with her left arm wrapped around the broom and the handle of the dustpan gripped with the thumb and two other fingers of her right hand, making her rethink that decision. She could call Megan, of course. Her sister had developed the drug she was taking and would know whether it was safe to take the painkiller she'd been prescribed.

But then she'd have to tell her sister about the fifteen stitches and Megan would insist on coming over to see for herself that it wasn't a fatal wound. And as much as she enjoyed spending time with her sister, she hated knowing that her family was still so worried about her. As they'd been worrying since she'd ended her engagement.

Because worrying translated into hovering, and while Ashley was still adjusting to living alone, she enjoyed having her own space. She ate her meals on her own schedule, watched whatever she wanted to watch on TV and generally came and went as she pleased without being accountable to anyone else.

Of course that would change when she had a baby, but she looked forward to the duties and responsibilities of motherhood. She wanted nothing more than to feel the stirring of a new life in her womb, and the warmth of a tiny baby in her arms.

Which was another reason she didn't want to fill the prescription Cam had written for her. Her appointment at the Pinehurst clinic was only a few days away and she didn't want anything to delay the start of the process. So she'd stick with her extra-strength Tylenol and hope that was enough to take the edge off of the pain.

Her stomach growled as she emptied the dustpan into the garbage, so she propped the broom and pan in the corner and moved to the fridge. Unfortunately, she found nothing that appealed to her. Or maybe she just didn't want to tackle putting together a meal with only one hand.

She could, however, dial the phone, and she was thinking about doing just that when the doorbell rang.

She'd never been the type to ignore a ringing phone and the echo of a bell had the same effect. She pulled open the door and, for the second time that day, found herself facing her past.

"Making house calls, Dr. Turcotte?" she asked him. Her

tone was deliberately casual, refusing to acknowledge the jump in her pulse.

For as far back as she could remember, her body had always instinctively reacted to Cameron's presence. Since she could do nothing about that response, she simply tried to ignore it.

But she couldn't deny that he looked good. His hair was as dark as she remembered, and still long enough to flirt with the collar of his shirt. His eyes were the same rich green that brought to mind the Irish countryside of her ancestors, and his gaze was just as intense. The shadow on his jaw attested to a long day at the office and gave him a slightly dangerous edge. Dangerously sexy, she mused, and immediately pushed the thought aside.

He had on the same shirt and khaki pants he'd been wearing earlier, but he'd loosened the knot in his tie and rolled up his sleeves, revealing darkly tanned and strongly muscled forearms. He used to be an avid tennis player and she found herself wondering if he still enjoyed pounding a fuzzy yellow ball around the court. It would certainly explain his trim and toned physique.

"Actually, I'm not here in my professional capacity," he told her, his comment drawing her back from her perusal.

"Then why are you here?" She knew the question sounded rude, but she didn't care. She was tired, her hand ached and she didn't have the energy or the desire to put a smile on her face, though she was suddenly experiencing an unwelcome stirring of certain other desires.

Cam lifted a flat white box that she hadn't even noticed he was carrying because she'd been too busy looking at him.

"Pizza delivery," he said.

"I didn't order pizza."

"And yet I've got a large double pepperoni and extra cheese in my hands."

It was her favorite kind. Of course, it had always been his favorite, too. Had he remembered her preference? Or had he just ordered it the way he liked it?

Not that it mattered. Even if he had remembered, their history was exactly that, and she wasn't going to let his sudden appearance at her door drag her down memory lane.

So all she asked was, "Why?"

He shrugged. "Because I worked through lunch and I was hungry, and because I figured it would be difficult for you to put together dinner for yourself with those stitches in your hand."

It sounded not only reasonable but thoughtful, and she was undeniably tempted to invite him in. There was something about Cam Turcotte that had always tempted her, but she wasn't a teenager anymore and she had no intention of letting down any of her barriers where he was concerned.

"I'm not hungry," she lied.

"You should eat anyway."

Still, she hesitated. "Contrary to whatever Irene might have told you, I don't need anyone looking out for me, Dr. Turcotte."

"It's just a pizza, Ash."

He was using his doctor tone again, patient and reasonable, and she knew that she was being anything but reasonable.

As he said, it was just a pizza. And she was hungry.

She stepped back from the door.

"Fine. Bring in the pizza."

Her welcome left something to be desired.

As Cam stepped into the foyer, he wondered again why he was there when it was readily apparent that Ashley wished he wasn't. He'd known he was taking a chance when he looked up her address in the file, but he'd never been able to think clearly when it came to Ashley Roarke.

"Nice neighborhood," he said, conversationally.

"We like it."

"We?" he queried, following her through to the kitchen.

"Megan and I bought the house a couple of years ago and lived here together until she got married. I guess I haven't quite got used to being on my own yet."

"I thought you were talking about the fiancé," he admitted, setting the pizza box in the middle of the table.

"*Ex*-fiancé," she clarified.

She opened the cupboard to get plates, but he reached over her head for them so that she didn't have to stretch.

"Yeah. I got that from what Irene said," he admitted.

"You mean she didn't give you the whole sordid story?"

"Is it sordid?"

She shrugged as she moved toward the refrigerator. "Let's just say he didn't think the act of putting a ring on my finger mandated exclusivity."

"Bastard," Cam said.

Ashley smiled, appreciating his unequivocal assessment and deciding that she might enjoy his company after all.

"The official term, at least among my friends, is 'cheating bastard,'" she told him.

"I'm sorry, Ash. You deserved better than that."

"Well, as Paige likes to remind me, at least I found out *before* we got married."

"I don't imagine that was much consolation."

"No," she admitted, peering into the refrigerator. "Beer, wine or soft drink?"

"Beer would be great."

She snagged a bottle for him and a soft drink for herself and carried the beverages to the table.

Again, before she could ask for help, Cam had both of the drinks open.

His unsolicited assistance reminded her of the days when they'd been dating, when he'd somehow been able to anticipate what she wanted without her saying a word. Like instinctively knowing the type of movie she wanted to see on a given night, or whether she preferred to stay home rather than go out. Bringing her flowers to brighten her day when she hadn't even known she was feeling down, or stopping by simply to spend time with her before she'd acknowledged that she was lonely.

Just like tonight, she realized now, and felt a funny little flutter in the vicinity of her heart.

She picked up the soda he'd opened for her and took a long swallow. She didn't want to be feeling any flutters, not now and definitely not because of Cam Turcotte.

"Premium beer," Cam noted appreciatively, picking up his bottle.

"My brother-in-law's company," she said, gratefully latching on to the neutral topic.

"That's right." He lifted a slice of pizza and slid it onto her plate before taking another one for himself. "Your sister married Gage Richmond. I read about his career change—and their marriage—in a business magazine somewhere."

"The Richmond name always makes good copy." She pulled a piece of pepperoni off of her pizza and popped it into her mouth.

"Megan works at Richmond Pharmaceuticals, doesn't she?"

She nodded. "Recently promoted to VP of clinical science."

"Impressive."

"No kidding. Whenever she tries to talk to me about something she's doing at work, my eyes glaze over."

"As I'm sure her eyes glaze when you want to discuss the intrinsic value of finger painting."

She smiled at that. "Very few people over the age of ten appreciate the intrinsic value of finger painting," she told him.

"But with Megan, it's not that she doesn't understand, just that she has an irrational fear of any human being less than three feet tall."

"I take it she doesn't plan on having kids then?"

"Not anytime in the near future," she said, then realized she was no longer certain it was true. After all, her sister was married now and starting a family with her new husband wasn't outside the realm of possibility. She pushed the thought—and the irrational spurt of envy—aside.

"I appreciate the pizza," she said. "But why are you really here?"

"I just wanted to see you, to talk to you, without an audience."

"Why?"

"For a lot of reasons," he said. "But primarily because we're living in the same town again, which means our paths are going to cross on occasion, and I don't want things to be awkward between us."

"Our paths are only crossing now because you showed up at my door."

He helped himself to another slice of pizza. "Actually, my door is just down the street."

She frowned. "Excuse me?"

"Number fifty-eight. The SOLD sign on the front lawn."

The pizza in Ashley's stomach suddenly felt like a ball of lead. "*You* bought that house?"

"The rent they were asking was astronomical," he said, as if that was a perfectly logical response to her question.

"I can't believe you bought it," she said.

But what she was thinking was that she was completely unprepared to be neighbors with her ex-lover. It was one thing to accept that he'd returned to Pinehurst—it was a big enough town that she wasn't likely to run into him at the grocery store very often—and quite another to know that he would be living just down the street and that she would have to pass by his house every single day on the way to and from her own.

"I thought you weren't sure this was a permanent move, that's why you wanted a one-year contract …" She let the words trail off, realizing she'd already said too much, admitted too much.

"You asked Elijah about me," he guessed.

She shrugged, an implicit admission that she'd done just that after Paige had warned her of Cam's impending return. "I was curious about the rumors that you were coming back. It's not like he violated any doctor-patient privilege by confirming it was true."

"Curious in a good way?" he asked her.

She lifted her hand to brush her hair away from her face, winced. "Just curious."

Cam frowned at the expression of discomfort. "Are you still experiencing pain?"

"A little."

"You shouldn't have any with the meds I prescribed."

She didn't say anything.

"You did take the medication, didn't you?" he prompted.

"No," she admitted.

"Why not?"

She shrugged. "I don't like taking anything stronger than over-the-counter drugs."

"Honey, you didn't come into the office because you had a headache, you had fifteen stitches put in your hand."

"I'm fine," she said. "And don't call me 'honey.'"

"You didn't object to Irene calling you 'hon,'" he pointed out.

She didn't say anything.

"Or was that okay because she hasn't seen you naked?"

Ashley blushed at the reminder that *he* had seen her naked, as he knew she would, but tilted her chin. "Actually, Irene has seen me naked."

He lifted his brows.

"But not since I was in diapers," she admitted, and gave him a small smile.

She'd always been beautiful. But when she smiled, when the light of humor sparked in the depths of her violet eyes and those soft pink lips curved, she was absolutely radiant.

Sitting across the table from her now, looking at her over a pizza box, he wondered how he'd ever settled for anything less, how he'd ever believed that his feelings for anyone else could compare to the emotion that filled his heart when he was with Ashley.

His gaze locked with hers, held. And suddenly the air was sizzling with the attraction that had always sparked between them.

"Did you have those five freckles at the base of your spine when you were in diapers?" he asked.

He could tell by the darkening of her eyes that mention of those freckles had stirred memories for her, too.

"I don't know," she said softly.

"Do you still have them?"

"I don't know," she said again.

Obviously the ex-fiancé had never kissed each and every one of those freckles, as Cam used to do. But he wasn't going to mention the other man's name again. He didn't even want to think about her being with anyone else. He wanted—

The scrape of chair legs against the floor tiles severed his thought as Ashley pushed her chair away from the table. Which was probably for the best, because he had no business thinking about what he wanted to do with Ashley when so much of his life was still unsettled.

"I should, uh, clear this up," she said.

He carried the plates into the kitchen for her, and pulled out the waste basket to scrape them before loading the dishwasher. But he paused when he saw what was in the receptacle.

"I'm guessing this is the eleven-by-fourteen," he said.

"What?" She turned around, saw that he'd found the broken picture frame. "Oh. Yeah. It is."

"It's a good picture of you," he said. "You look happy."

She shrugged. "I was."

And the man in the photo with her looked happy, too. Of course, he had Ashley in his arms, so he had reason to be happy. Which made Cam realize her former fiancé wasn't just a bastard, he was an idiot. He'd been poised to start a life with this beautiful, vibrant woman, and he'd thrown it away.

Okay, so maybe he was being a little bit hypocritical. Because twelve years earlier, Ashley had wanted to talk about their future and he'd let her go. But he'd barely been nineteen years old, too young to be thinking in terms of "till death do us part" and too stupid to know what he was giving up.

Cam picked up his beer, took a long swallow. "Are you still in love with him?"

Ashley returned the unused napkins to the holder then leaned back against the counter. "How is that any of your business?"

"When a man kisses a woman it's important to his ego—crucial, in fact—to know that she's thinking of him and not anyone else."

She eyed him warily. "If a man doesn't know that about a woman, then he has no business kissing her."

"That's why I asked the question." He set the now empty bottle on the counter and stepped closer to her, bracing his hands on the edge of the counter so that she was boxed between them. "Are you still in love with him?"

* * *

Ashley didn't dare answer his question with the truth.

The truth was, she was no longer convinced she'd ever been in love with Trevor. Certainly she hadn't loved him as she should have loved the man she was planning to marry. But if she admitted that to Cam now, he would interpret it as an invitation and, as desperately as she wanted to feel his mouth on hers, she couldn't let that happen.

Because she knew that one kiss would lead to more, and she didn't want more. She'd meant what she said when she told Megan and Paige that she didn't want a man or a relationship. She didn't want to risk her heart again.

"Yes," she said.

"Yes what?"

"Yes, I still love…" Oh Lord, she couldn't even remember his name. She could only think of Cam. She only wanted Cam. "…I still love him."

"Liar."

The word was a husky whisper against her lips before he captured them with his own.

She couldn't stop herself from responding to his kiss any more than she could stop her heart from pounding or her body from yearning. His tongue traced over the seam of her lips, and they parted willingly, eagerly.

It seemed to her that they'd grown too far apart to fit together easily. The moment he slipped his arms around her and drew her against him, she knew she'd been wrong.

Cam had always been a fabulous kisser. When they'd first started dating, back in the early days of their relationship when they hadn't gone any further than kissing, he would hold her and kiss her forever. This kiss reminded her of that—as if it would go on forever, as if he could be content to just kiss her forever.

Ashley wasn't feeling content. She pressed against him, wanting to be closer, wanting more.

His hands slid up her back, his fingers tangled in her hair, and he drew her head back. His mouth trailed from hers to trace along her jaw, down her throat. His tongue stroked, his teeth scraped, his lips soothed.

He shifted, drew her nearer, so that she was nestled intimately between his legs, so that she could tell he wanted her as much as she wanted him. Desire—hot and reckless—churned in her veins, rushed through her body, making her feel as if she was seventeen years old again.

Of course, her teenage heart had been filled with more love than lust, and though she'd given herself to him willingly, even eagerly, she'd been unprepared for the complete and total heartbreak that was all he'd left her with when he went away.

A heartbreak that, at the time, she didn't ever think she would recover from. A heartbreak that she'd felt even deeper and sharper than the pain caused by Trevor's betrayal.

She'd loved Cam once and he'd trampled all over her emotions. She wouldn't let him do it again. She didn't want to feel anything for the man who'd broken her fragile heart so many years before.

But as she kissed him back, she couldn't deny that she was feeling something, though she didn't know how to define what that something was.

Attraction? Undoubtedly. Cam Turcotte had been a teenage heartthrob, and the years had added to rather than detracted from his appeal.

Lust? No doubt a healthy dose of that had been thrown into the mix. And maybe that wasn't surprising, considering that she was a twenty-nine-year-old woman who hadn't been on a date since the end of her engagement.

She'd had offers. When she'd gone out with Paige and

Megan or friends from work, she'd been approached by men who expressed an interest. But she hadn't even been tempted. In fact, she hadn't felt anything but numb for so long she didn't know what to think about the feelings that were spiraling through her now.

When would she ever learn?

Obviously the trauma of slicing open her hand had affected her brain. It was the only explanation for letting him kiss her, for letting the kiss go as far as it did.

He'd caught her in a moment of weakness, but she was drawing the line, right here and right now. She would not get caught up in the seductive magnetism of Cam Turcotte. Not again.

She had to end this now—that would be the smart thing to do. But it felt so good to be held and kissed and…cherished.

Except that he didn't cherish her. He never had. Because if he'd truly treasured her and what they had together, he wouldn't have walked away so easily.

Which was why, this time, she had to be the one to walk.

She tore her mouth from his and pushed against his chest.

Chapter Four

Ashley stumbled back and cried out in pain. The obvious distress in her voice effectively doused Cam's raging libido. He drew in a slow, deep breath then reached for her hand. She shook her head and took another step back, as if she couldn't bear to have him touch her.

He didn't know what he'd done to make her withdraw so abruptly and completely, but he wasn't thinking about that at the moment. He was thinking about the fact that her eyes were clouded with pain now rather than lust, and he worried that she might have re-injured her hand.

"I just want to make sure that you're not bleeding again," he told her.

This time when he reached for her hand, she didn't object. He carefully peeled back the gauze to check the wound, pleased to see that none of the stitches had opened up.

"It looks okay," he said, refastening the tape.

She nodded.

"But I want to know why you're not taking the painkillers when it's obvious that you're in pain."

"I told you, I don't like taking any medication unnecessarily."

Ashley had never been practiced in the art of deception, and the fact that she didn't look at him when she spoke told him more clearly than her words that there was something she was holding back.

"If you're hurting, it's necessary," he insisted.

"I'm fine."

"What medications are you taking that you didn't want to tell me about?"

The question was a stab in the dark, but her lack of response made him believe it had been an accurate one.

"We can argue back and forth for another few minutes if you really want," he told her. "But I'm not backing off until you tell me."

"Fedentropin," she finally said.

He frowned. "I'm not familiar with that one."

"It's an experimental drug to help alleviate the symptoms of endometriosis. I'm part of a clinical trial at Richmond Pharmaceuticals."

"I didn't realize…" He wasn't sure what he meant to say, what was the right thing to say. He'd had no idea that she had to endure what he knew was a painful and chronic condition for a woman, and he hated to think of her suffering.

But Ashley just shrugged. "It's not something that comes up in conversation."

"It should have been noted in your file," he said.

"Eli knows—I talked to him before I was accepted into the test group, but I haven't had an appointment with him since."

Cam believed there still should have been a note in her file, but right now he was more concerned about her current situation. "Is your sister running the trial?"

She nodded.

He picked up the cordless phone on the counter. "Call her."

"Why?"

"I want to know if you can take the medication I prescribed or if I should write a scrip for something else."

"Look, Cam, I appreciate your concern, but I took some Tylenol when I got home and I'm okay."

She wouldn't have cried out in pain if she was okay and since he figured they were both aware of that fact, he only asked, "Why don't you want to call your sister?"

"Why won't you back off?" she countered.

"Because I care about you."

Maybe he was surprised by the admission, but not by the feelings. He *did* care about Ashley. He'd always cared about Ashley.

She turned away from him, but not before he saw the glint of tears in her eyes.

"You have no right," she said, her tone laced with both hurt and anger. "No right to barge into my life after *twelve years* and make such a statement as if it gives you the right to interfere."

It was true. He'd given up any right he might have had when he'd ended their relationship a dozen years earlier. But his feelings for Ashley had never been rational, and even when he'd gone away, his feelings for her never had.

"I've always cared about you, Ash, and I always will."

She turned away to wrap up the leftover pizza, struggling a little because of her bandaged hand. "Thank you for your concern," she said, not sounding thankful at all. "Now go away."

He knew he should. But instead, Cam scrolled through the list of numbers stored in the memory of the phone still in his hand.

"What are you doing?" she demanded.

He found "Megan & Gage" and pressed the call button. "Calling your sister."

She stared at him, as if she didn't really believe he'd do it.

"It's ringing," he warned her.

She grabbed the phone with her uninjured hand. As obviously unhappy as she was about making the call, she seemed to accept that he would talk directly to Megan if she continued to refuse and had likely concluded that her sister would have fewer questions for her than she would for him.

After a brief conversation, during which she reassured her sister numerous times that she was fine and didn't need anyone coming over to check up on her, Ashley said goodbye and disconnected.

"*That's* why I didn't want to call her," she said.

"Because you knew she'd be worried about you?" he asked, wondering why her sister's concern should be a problem for Ashley.

"Because she's spent too much time worrying about me, and even more over the past four months."

"Since the broken engagement," he guessed.

She nodded, making him suspect that she might be more distressed over the end of that relationship than he wanted to believe. And though he was undeniably curious about the ex-fiancé, he forced himself to focus on more immediate concerns.

"What did Megan say about the medication?"

"She said it's fine. I just have to make sure that I inform the admin clerk of the dosage when I go in for my blood work."

"Except you didn't get the scrip filled, did you?"

"No, because I didn't plan on taking it."

He glanced at his watch. "I'll call it in to Brody's."

"I'm capable of taking my own prescription in."

"I know you are," he agreed. "I'm just not convinced that you'll actually do it."

"Fine." She thrust the phone at him. "Call it in and then leave me alone."

He dialed the familiar number, spoke to the pharmacist and made arrangements for the medication to be delivered, throughout which Ashley continued to glare at him.

"It should be here within twenty minutes," he told her.

"Do you plan on hanging around until it gets here?" she challenged.

"I don't have anywhere else that I need to be, and I have no intention of letting you push me out the door until we've had a chance to talk about what happened in the kitchen."

"There's nothing to talk about," she denied, but the flush in her cheeks told him otherwise. "It was a moment of insanity, that's all."

"The only insanity is in trying to pretend it didn't mean anything, trying to pretend that we aren't still as attracted to one another as we were twelve years ago."

She folded her arms over her chest as she lifted her gaze to his. "I'm not going to deny that there's an attraction, but I'm not looking to get involved with anyone right now."

A personal relationship was the absolute last thing he'd been looking for when he'd decided to move back to Pinehurst, but then he'd kissed Ashley, and he'd realized that getting involved with her wasn't a choice. But he understood why she was wary.

"You can't close your heart because of what your ex-fiancé did," he said gently.

"This had nothing to do with Trevor," she denied.

"I'd say the picture in your trash can suggests otherwise."

"You're right," she decided. "This has *everything* to do with Trevor. Because if he hadn't chosen to send that picture to me, I wouldn't have sliced my hand and you wouldn't have needed to stitch it up, and you definitely wouldn't be here right now."

"Then maybe I should thank Trevor," he said.

She glared at him. "In any event, I have no intention of picking up our relationship where we left off just because it's convenient for you now."

He felt his own anger stir. "My feelings for you were a lot of things," he told her. "But convenient was never one of them."

As soon as her prescription was delivered, Ashley took the requisite pills and sent Cam on his way.

From the moment she'd returned from her shopping trip earlier in the day, nothing had gone according to plan. Coming face-to-face with Cam had been unexpected, but it had also been unavoidable. Especially since he would be moving in down the street.

So while their meeting was inevitable, she'd been confident that when they did meet, they would simply exchange a few coolly polite words and go their separate ways. She certainly hadn't expected anything like the kiss they'd shared in her kitchen.

Because while Cam might have made the first move, there was no denying that she'd been an equal—and willing—participant.

Yeah, that kiss had definitely been a mistake, because now she was dealing with the aftermath—a jumble of feelings that she hadn't been prepared for and didn't know what to do with.

It had only been one kiss. Nothing that should have the power to turn her world upside down. But it felt as if that was exactly what had happened.

He'd been absent from her life for twelve years but somehow, after only a few hours, he'd managed to churn up all kinds of feelings and desires that she'd buried a long time ago. Or so she'd thought.

She sorted through the mail, opened the cupboard under the sink to drop the flyers into the recycle box and saw that a new bag had been put in the garbage can. Cam must have taken out the other bag for her—the one with the broken picture frame and her engagement photo in it.

Because he thought seeing the photo again might upset her? Or because he thought she was clumsy enough to injure herself again when she took the bag out?

She closed the cupboard and sighed. She had no idea what Cam's reasons were. She didn't know anything at all about him anymore. And yet, there was something still there between them. Something that both thrilled and terrified her.

It had been easy for her to toss the picture of her fiancé into the garbage, because she had closed the door on that part of her life with no regrets. She *had* been happy with Trevor, at least for a while, and she'd wanted the life they had planned to build together. But the truth was, she'd never loved him as completely and wholeheartedly as she'd loved Cam.

It was an unsettling realization, and one she wasn't ready to examine too closely. Determined to push the sexy doctor out of her mind, she went upstairs to get ready for bed.

The sun hadn't yet set, but she was exhausted—physically and emotionally—and she wanted nothing more than to crawl between the sheets and sink into oblivion where thoughts and memories of Cam Turcotte didn't exist.

Cam was surprised to find his parents' car in the driveway when he got back to their house after his detour to Ashley's. He walked through the back door and followed the trail of an enticingly spicy scent into the kitchen where his mother was stirring something on the stove.

"I thought tonight was your bowling night," he said in lieu of a greeting.

"Your dad spent the afternoon at Harry Reiner's, helping him lay patio stones," Gayle told her son.

"He screwed up his back again, didn't he?"

"He's in bed with an ice pack now," she confirmed.

"Why does he do things like that?"

"Because Harry helped stain our deck, and your dad insisted that this was his way of returning the favor."

"A paintbrush doesn't weigh forty pounds," Cam noted.

His mother smiled. "Which is exactly what I said to him. But then I made the mistake of noting that he's also several years older than Harry, which he interpreted as a challenge."

"Because it drives him crazy the way Harry flirts with you."

"Harry's been widowed for nearly ten years, he's lonely, and he flirts with every woman who crosses his path." She finished scooping chili into a bowl. "Do you want some?"

"Oh. No, thanks. I had a couple of slices of pizza earlier."

She carried her bowl to the table and sat down. "Is everything okay?"

"Sure. Why?"

"Because you're a lot later than usual getting home and you seem a little distracted."

"Busy day at the office." He helped himself to a bottle of beer from the fridge and sat down with her.

He'd moved in with them when he'd returned to Pinehurst because it was convenient and gave him the opportunity to look for a place of his own. What had surprised him was how much he'd enjoyed spending time with them. After living so far away for so many years, it was nice to reconnect again, and to realize that he actually liked his parents.

"That's why Elijah needed to hire you," she said. "So what was different about today?"

He took a long swallow from the bottle. "I saw Ashley."

She paused, her spoon halfway to her lips. "Ashley Roarke?"

He nodded.

"How did that go?"

He thought about their kiss—the soft responsiveness of her lips, the yielding warmth of her body—and her abrupt and complete withdrawal from him. "Better—and worse—than I expected."

"I'm...sorry?"

He smiled. "I guess I shouldn't have expected that she'd be happy about my decision to come back to Pinehurst now."

"I would think, if her feelings for you are well and truly gone, she wouldn't have much of an opinion one way or the other."

He mulled that over for a minute. "The implication being that if she cares, she must still have feelings for me?"

"Twelve years is a long time, and you were both so young when you went away. And yet—" she smiled "—a woman never forgets her first love."

"Spoken like a woman with fond memories," he noted.

"I fell in love when I was fifteen—much to the chagrin of both my parents and his. He was nearly twenty, already in college, and our families were united only in their desire to keep us apart."

"What happened?"

Her eyes sparkled. "I married him."

"Grandma and Grandpa disapproved of Dad?" He couldn't believe it. His father was the epitome of responsibility and respectability—certainly not the usual type that parents warned their daughters about.

"I was fifteen," she said again. "I don't think they would have approved of anyone I brought home at that age. And he was so...sexy. He worked in construction in the summer to earn money for college and he had all these rippling muscles and—"

"Please." Cam held up a hand, urging her to spare him the details.

"If I hadn't been attracted to your father, you wouldn't be here," she pointed out.

"Still, there are some things a kid doesn't need to know."

"Well, my point," she said, "is that parents always want what they think is best for their kids, even when it conflicts with what their kids want. That's why your dad encouraged you to go away to school, to put some distance between you and Ashley before you got too deeply involved."

"He knew how I felt about her."

She nodded. "And he was afraid that you'd give up your dreams to stay in Pinehurst with her."

"Why did he think that?" he asked curiously. "Was there something he felt he'd missed out on by getting married so young?"

His mother was silent for a long minute before she said, "He wasn't thinking about his own dreams, but mine."

It had never occurred to him that his mom might have sacrificed her own plans to be a wife and a mother, because she'd always seemed so settled and content in those roles. "What was your dream?" he asked her now.

"After I met your dad, I only wanted to be with him."

But he recognized the evasion, and his curiosity was piqued. "Before you met Dad?" he prompted.

"I was going to be a doctor," she finally admitted.

He shouldn't have been surprised, but he was. He couldn't believe that he'd never known his mother had once envisioned having the same career that he'd chosen for himself.

"A doctor," he echoed.

She nodded. "In fact, I'd just been accepted to medical school when I found out I was pregnant."

He set his now empty bottle down. "You gave up your dream because of me?"

But she shook her head vehemently. "No. By the time I got pregnant, my dream had changed. Finding out that I was going to have a baby was the most incredible moment of my life. I had no qualms about giving up medical school for motherhood.

"But when you first expressed an interest in becoming a doctor, your father was adamant that nothing would cause you to make the sacrifice he believed I'd made. But what he didn't think about—what neither of us really considered—was what would make you happy."

"You shouldn't worry about that anymore," he assured her. "I am happy."

"A parent always worries. Especially when her kids grow up and move away."

He knew she wasn't just thinking of him, but of his younger sister, Sherry, who was now married and living in Florida.

"Well, I have no doubt that you would have been a great doctor," he said. "But you made the right career choice, because you are definitely the world's greatest mom."

She smiled through the sheen of tears in her eyes. "And when a mother's grown son says something like that, she knows she's done her job well."

When Ashley returned to the doctor's office for her follow-up appointment, she was prepared to see Cam. Not just to see him, but to prove that she was completely unaffected by him, that the scorching kiss they'd shared in her kitchen meant nothing to her. Less than nothing, in fact.

When the door opened, however, it wasn't Cam who came in—it was Eli. She felt a slight pang but assured herself it wasn't disappointment. After all, it wasn't that she wanted to see Cam except to prove that he didn't mean anything to her. Not anymore.

But Eli meant the world to her, and her smile came easily for him.

"How's Ruby?" she asked, having learned about his wife's heart attack from Megan, who worked with one of the doctor's neighbors.

"She's doing well. Thanks for the beautiful flowers. She was so tickled that you remembered gerberas are her favorite."

"I was hoping they would brighten up her room and her spirits."

"The did both," Eli confirmed. "And remarkably well, I'd say, since she's scheduled to come home tomorrow."

"You must be so relieved."

He nodded. "We've been married forty-two years. After that much time, you start to take certain things for granted. But I'm not taking anything for granted anymore."

Ashley wondered if she would ever know that kind of deep and abiding love, and realized that she still hoped she would. She hadn't completely given up on the idea of finding someone to share her life, she'd just decided not to worry about doing so. And, in the meantime, she would happily lavish all of her love and attention on the baby she was going to have.

"But I know you didn't really come here to talk abut me," the doctor continued. "So tell me how you're doing."

"I'm anxious to get these stitches out," she admitted.

He scanned the notes in her file, closed the folder and reached for her hand. "Let's take a look then."

While he was bent over her hand, she stared at the calendar on the wall on the opposite side of the room, breathing slowly and carefully as she silently calculated the days and then the hours and minutes until it was time to go back to school. She felt a few little tugs, but no pain, and as long as she didn't think about the fact that he was pulling threads out of her hand, she didn't feel dizzy.

She hadn't felt anything when Cam put the stitches in, either. Of course, she'd been given an injection to freeze the site, but even without the artificial numbing, she knew her awareness of Cam would have eclipsed everything else.

"How does it feel?"

She glanced down, saw that he'd finished removing the stitches. She carefully curled her fingers into a fist, nodded. "It feels good."

"Cam did a nice job," Eli said. "In a few more weeks, the scar will barely be visible."

Ashley uncurled her fist and was pleased to note that there was no residual pain in her hand.

If only the same could be said about the scars Cam had left on her heart twelve years earlier.

Chapter Five

As a child, Ashley had always looked forward to the first day of school. As a teacher, she still did.

Maybe it would be different if she taught high school, where the students were more sullen and jaded. But for a group of five- and six-year-olds, entering first grade was as thrilling an event as Columbus's discovery of a whole new world. They were all so young and eager to learn, and Ashley found their excitement and enthusiasm never failed to recharge her own.

She didn't usually have supervision duty on Wednesday mornings, but like most other teachers on staff at Parkdale Elementary School, it was a tradition to meet on the playground behind the school so the students could catch a glimpse of their teachers before they entered the classroom, and vice versa. She knew most of the kids who would be in her class, of course, because the majority had attended kindergarten at the same school the previous year. But there were always a few new faces, children who had moved into the neighborhood over the summer and who were even more anxious about the first day because everything was strange and unfamiliar.

It was easy to spot the new ones, and Ashley liked to introduce herself before the first bell and to meet with the mother who was usually present and in whose hand a much smaller one would be tightly clasped.

She had three new students this year and she'd already made the rounds to say hello and invite the parents to come into the classroom. Some would accept her offer and, in doing so, would feel reassured about the environment in which they'd left their children. Others would decline, knowing that it would only make saying goodbye that much more difficult for the child. Ashley was supportive of either decision, trusting that the parent knew his or her child better than she did—at least on the first day.

She smiled at Adam Webber, one of the fifth-grade teachers and the boys' basketball coach, when he came out of the school with the ever-present orange ball tucked under his arm.

"Look at them." Adam shook his head. "So eager and enthusiastic."

"Don't worry, you'll beat that out of them soon enough."

He grinned easily at her teasing, because he knew he was one of the favorite teachers at Parkdale. "How does your class look this year? Or should I wait until the end of the day to ask you?"

"Twenty-three kids. Ten boys, thirteen girls."

"Twenty-four," he said.

"What?"

"Haven't you seen Wendy this morning?" Adam asked, referring to the principal's administrative assistant.

"No, I came directly around the back."

"She told me she has an updated class list for you."

"But I just picked up the list yesterday. And I did all of the name tags and locker magnets last night."

He shrugged. "I'm just the messenger."

Ashley turned to go into the school, and that's when she saw her.

The child looked the right age for a first grader, with long, dark hair and wide, terrified eyes. She was wearing a sleeveless pink dress with tiny white daisies embroidered at the square neckline and along the hem, with matching pink canvas sneakers embroidered with the same flowers on the toes.

Obviously the newest addition.

Feeling an instinctive stir of empathy, Ashley had already started forward when she glanced from the child to parent—and froze.

The man holding the little girl's hand was Cam Turcotte.

Ashley stopped by Wendy's office and grabbed the new class list before ducking into her classroom and closing the door at her back. She just needed five minutes alone. Five minutes to assimilate the reality that had been shoved in her face. Five minutes to accept that Cam had a child—that the baby she'd once dreamed of having with him had been born to someone else.

She didn't want to believe it. And yet she couldn't deny it was true. There was no doubt the little girl with the shiny dark hair and wide green eyes clinging to his hand as if he was the center of her world could be anyone but his daughter.

But how could she not have known?

Cam might have moved away more than twelve years ago, but his parents had remained in town. In fact, it had been from his mother that she'd heard about his marriage to Danica, and that news had hit her the same way.

Gayle Turcotte, apparently recognizing how much the

revelation had hurt Ashley, had been careful not to make any further mention of her son's life in Seattle whenever their paths had crossed. She'd certainly never mentioned the baby girl that Cam's wife had given birth to.

Madeline Carrington-Turcotte, according to the updated class list she'd inadvertently crumpled in her fist.

Cam had always been very traditional, so she would bet that the hyphenated name was his ex-wife's idea. Just because Ashley had been foolish enough to doodle "Ashley Turcotte" inside the cover of her notebooks when she was in high school didn't mean another woman would feel the same way about taking her husband's name.

In any event, she and Cam had broken up more than twelve years earlier, so she knew it was ridiculous to feel so hurt by the knowledge that he'd had a child with another woman. But that knowledge failed to lessen her sense of betrayal.

Because when Cam had left her, one of the reasons he'd given for ending their relationship was that he didn't want the life she'd envisioned for them—not yet.

"I've decided to go to Seattle," he told her.

Ashley stared at him, feeling as if the very ground beneath her feet had begun to crumble. "Washington?"

He nodded. "Their School of Medicine is one of the best in the country."

"But—" She didn't quite know what to say, how to respond to something that he'd obviously already decided upon, and without even discussing it with her "—but you have at least three years before med school."

"I know. But staying here, going to a university closer to home, it will only delay the inevitable."

Inevitable? *What was it that he thought was inevitable?*

Ashley didn't ask, because in her heart, she was afraid she already knew the answer. But she pushed aside her fears.

"There are good medical schools that aren't on the other side of the country. Like Northwestern and Cornell. Even Chapel Hill would be better than Washington."

"I want to go to Washington."

She'd heard the finality in his voice, and her eyes had filled with tears. "You're breaking up with me."

He glanced away. "This is for the best, Ash."

"Best for who?" she demanded.

"For both of us. Do you think this was an easy decision for me to make?"

"How would I know—since you never talked to me about it?"

"Because I knew you would try to convince me to stay. And because I was afraid I would let you." He reached out and took her hands. "Because there's a part of me that wants nothing more than to stay here with you."

The seemingly heartfelt words and the warmth of his touch failed to thaw the icy numbness that had taken hold of her.

She managed to speak, though she didn't manage to disguise the anguish in her tone when she asked, "Then why are you leaving?"

"Because we want different things, Ash. Being a doctor has been my dream for as long as I can remember."

"You said you wanted to get married."

"I do," he agreed. "Someday. But I'm nowhere near being ready to make that kind of commitment yet. I'm not even close to thinking about being a husband or a father."

As it turned out, that wasn't exactly true.

Because only a few years later, before Ashley had even graduated from teacher's college, he had married. He'd become someone else's husband. And now she knew that he'd become a father, too.

He'd had the family she always wanted, and she was still alone.

Ashley wiped the tears from her cheeks, reminding herself that she wasn't going to be alone forever. Despite her initial appointment at PARC having to be rescheduled, she *was* going to have a baby. And while she couldn't deny a certain amount of disappointment that her child wouldn't also have a father, she'd made her decision.

She wouldn't regret that the baby she'd so often dreamed of having with Cam Turcotte would never be. And she absolutely wouldn't let herself consider the possibility that his return to Pinehurst could change anything. Especially now that she knew he already was a father.

The ring of the bell jolted her out of her reverie. She hastily wiped the last of the moisture from her cheeks, pasted a smile on her face and opened the door to greet her new students.

She wasn't sure how she made it through the day, but when the bell sounded at three o'clock, Ashley nearly wept with relief.

It took a few more minutes, of course, to ensure all the kids had their agendas and the assortment of documents that always went home on the first day. But the halls eventually emptied and quiet descended, and Ashley sank back into her chair.

"One day down, only one hundred and eighty-something to go."

Ashley looked up, startled to see her sister in the doorway. Megan rarely ever came to the school to see Ashley, and the fact that she'd done so now indicated that she had something on her mind.

"One hundred and eighty-six," Ashley told her. "But what dragged you out of the lab in the middle of the day?"

Megan practically floated into the room. She wasn't usually the floating type, but she was obviously excited about something so Ashley tried to muster some enthusiasm for her.

"I had an appointment this side of town." Megan came

further into the room, some of the sparkle in her eyes fading as she looked more closely at her sister. "But let's talk about what's going on with you first."

Ashley shook her head. She couldn't talk about it. She didn't know what to say, how to explain.

"Come on, Ash. You love the first day of school. I thought you'd be ready to go out and celebrate the beginning of a new year with a great big chocolate fudge brownie sundae at Walton's."

"Let's just say that the day didn't go exactly as planned."

"I don't understand."

She sighed and pushed her class list across the desk. Megan picked up the page, frowning. Then her eyes widened.

"Madeline Carrington-Turcotte?"

Ashley nodded. "Cam's daughter."

"Oh, Ash."

"She's beautiful," she said softly. "And very sweet and shy. She doesn't say much, but she watches and she listens, her big green eyes taking everything in."

"Of all the classrooms in all the schools in all the world, she walks into yours."

Ashley managed to smile at the deliberate misquotation. "I just…I didn't know how to react. I was completely unprepared. I had no idea that he had a child, never mind one I would end up teaching."

"But he lives down the street," Megan reminded her. "You never saw her?"

She shook her head. "He only moved in on the weekend. I saw the truck, saw furniture being unloaded, but I didn't pay attention to anything else." And she was regretting that now.

"Chocolate fudge brownie sundae?" Meg prompted gently.

Ashley managed to smile. "That sounds like the perfect way to end a crappy day."

* * *

One of the reasons Cam had moved back to Pinehurst was to be able to spend more time with both his parents and his daughter. Another added benefit was that his parents were not just willing but happy to provide after-school care for Maddie on the days that he couldn't get away from the office in time to pick her up. But he refused to let her first day of school be one of those days, and when she came racing across the grass and into his arms, he was more certain than ever that this move was the best thing for both of them.

He felt a slight twinge when he recalled the shock—and the pain—he'd seen in Ashley's eyes when she saw him with Madeline that morning, and he realized the first-grade teacher might not agree. But he refused to worry about that while he walked home, hand in hand with his daughter, listening to her animated conversation the whole way.

He remembered her kindergarten teacher expressing concern that Maddie was too quiet in class, silent and with-drawn. But Cam knew it wasn't a character flaw, just her personality. She'd always been shy with strangers, but at home and with her family, she was quite the little chatterbox.

"Do you want a snack?" he asked.

"Ice cream," she said hopefully, hopping onto one of the stools at the breakfast bar.

"We don't have any."

She pouted. "You promised to get ice cream."

"I know I did, but I forgot."

His admission of guilt didn't appease her and though Cam knew the dangers of being over-indulgent, he figured the first day at a new school warranted an exception to the rules.

"So why don't you go wash up and we'll go to Walton's?"

"Who's Walton?"

He smiled. "Walton isn't a who but a where, and it's

where we go to get the very best ice cream in all of Pine-hurst, New York."

"Really?" Her eyes were almost as wide as her smile.

"Really."

She hopped off of her stool and wrapped her arms around his waist. "Thanks, Daddy. You're the best."

Twenty minutes later, he handed a strawberry sundae to Maddie before accepting his double scoop of butter pecan from the teenager behind the counter and turned to look for a vacant table. A quick glance around the room revealed that there weren't any.

"There's my teacher, Daddy."

Maddie's words registered at the exact moment his gaze landed on Ashley, seated with her sister at a table for four on the other side of the room.

"Her name's Miss Ashley," his daughter reminded him.

Cam nodded.

"She's very pretty," Maddie said. "And she smiles a lot and she doesn't yell. Not even when the skinny boy with the curly hair forgot to ask to go to the bathroom and went pee right in his pants."

His lips curved. "Not even then?"

Maddie shook her head solemnly.

"So maybe first grade won't be so bad, huh?"

"Maybe," she allowed. "But it's really too soon to tell."

He was smiling at her comment as he guided her toward Ashley and Megan's table.

"Looks like someone else decided to celebrate the first day of school with ice cream," Ashley noted, her attention and smile focused on Madeline.

"It seemed appropriate," Cam said.

"We thought the same thing," Megan said, when Ashley failed to respond to his comment.

"But there don't seem to be any vacant tables," he pointed out. "So we were hoping you wouldn't object to us joining you."

"Of course not," Megan said, though she cast a worried glance across the table.

Ashley still didn't say anything to him, but she slid across the bench she was sitting on to make room for his daughter. Maddie smiled shyly at her and carefully set her dish on the table before climbing up beside her teacher.

"Thanks," Cam said, taking the seat beside Megan. "I don't remember it ever being so busy in here."

"A lot changes in twelve years," Ashley told him.

He met her gaze across the table and felt the zing of sparks that weren't entirely attributable to her obvious annoyance with him.

"And some things," he countered, "never do."

Ashley ate her chocolate fudge brownie sundae so fast she was surprised she didn't get brain freeze. But from the moment she'd looked up and spotted Cam in line at the counter, she'd wanted only to get out of Walton's as quickly as possible. Thankfully her sister had sensed her discomfort and quickly finished her ice cream as well.

It was only after they'd said goodbye to Cam and Maddie and were on their way out the door that Ashley thought to ask again about the reasons for her sister's unexpected midweek visit.

Megan dumped her empty dish and spoon in the garbage. "It really wasn't that important."

"Important enough to bring you to the school to talk to me."

Her sister sighed. "Because I wanted to tell you first, but you've had a lot sprung on you already today."

And Ashley knew her sister's news and why she was suddenly reluctant to share it.

"You're pregnant," she guessed.

Meg nodded.

Ashley sucked in a breath.

Her sister was going to have a baby.

She felt a tug deep inside her heart. A combination of excitement and envy. She wanted to be happy for Megan. She was happy for her. And yet she couldn't help but look at the life her sister was building with her new husband and wonder why all of the stars had aligned so perfectly for Megan and, seemingly at the same time, scattered everything in her own world.

A little more than six months earlier, she and Paige had struggled to convince Megan that she had nothing to lose by inviting Gage Richmond to be her date for Ashley's engagement party. Megan had finally agreed, only because she'd been sure that Gage wouldn't accept. But he had and, even on that first date, Ashley had seen the chemistry between them. Even more significantly, she'd recognized that there was a connection between them that she didn't feel with the man she was planning to marry.

But she didn't let that dissuade her from her plans, because she believed that there were more important things than connections. There were shared interests and common goals. Or maybe she'd deluded herself into thinking she and Trevor had shared interests and common goals because she so desperately wanted to get married and have a family of her own.

She wasn't so desperate, however, that she was willing to overlook the fact that he'd been sleeping around on her almost from the time he'd put the ring on her finger. She'd been crushed to learn of his betrayal. And maybe, just a little, secretly relieved.

Because the closer the date had come for their wedding, the more she had started to realize that she was making a mistake. That she didn't love Trevor as much as she should love the man she intended to marry. That she didn't love him specifically as much as she loved the prospect of being a wife and mother.

Now Megan and Gage were married and getting ready to have a baby.

The tug came again. Stronger this time, but she pushed it aside. "Oh, Meg. That's wonderful news."

Her sister looked uncertain. "Are you really okay with this?"

"I'm thrilled for you," Ashley told her, willing it to be true. "I was just caught off guard by your announcement. I didn't even realize you and Gage were trying to have a baby."

"Well, we weren't actually trying, we just weren't trying to prevent it." She blushed prettily. "In fact, I think Gage is a little disappointed it happened as quickly as it did."

"Obviously you guys are doing something right," Ashley said.

Her sister's blush deepened. "*Everything* is right with Gage. I never thought I would feel this way about anyone— or that anyone else would feel the same way about me. But he's just—" her sigh was filled with blissful contentment "—amazing."

"So are you," Ashley told her sister. "Which is why you guys are so perfect for one another."

"That's what I want for you," Megan said. "I know Trevor's betrayal hit you hard, but you can't give up hope that you'll find someone to spend your life with just because of CBB."

"I haven't given up hope," Ashley said, though she wasn't entirely sure it was true. "I'm just not willing to put the rest of my life on hold while I wait around for Mr. Right to show up, because the reality is, there may not be a Mr. Right for me."

"There is," Megan insisted, and smiled slyly. "And I think he might already have shown up. Or maybe I should say shown up *again.*"

Ashley didn't bother to respond. Cam Turcotte was part of

her past, not her future, and she had no intention of arguing with her sister about that fact.

And no intention of letting herself yearn again for something that could never be.

Though it wasn't one of their scheduled evenings to get together, Ashley wasn't surprised when Paige showed up at her door Friday night. Or that she'd brought a bottle of her favorite merlot with her.

Ashley put together a platter of assorted crackers and cheeses and they took it out onto the porch with the wine.

"I don't know why you're paying rent on an apartment in Syracuse when you've been spending so much time in Pinehurst lately," Ashley said to her.

"I'm only here on the weekends," her cousin replied, glossing over the real issue. "Because it's too far to commute to the office every day."

"Seriously, Paige, what happened to your social life?"

Her cousin shrugged. "Things fizzled with Josh. Ben met someone else. As for Lucas—well, I realized I wasn't secure enough to date a guy who's prettier than me."

Ashley had met Lucas once, and while she had to admit the man was unbelievably good-looking, she knew that her cousin's serial dating was really a reflection of the nomadic childhood that had taught her, at an early age, not to form close attachments to people who wouldn't be in her life for very long. The pattern had changed only when Paige's father decided she needed more stability than his lifestyle afforded and finally left his daughter in the care of his sister and her husband. Ashley and Megan had forged an unbreakable bond with their cousin, but by habit or deliberation, she continued to keep everyone else at a distance.

"Is that why you're here?" Ashley asked her now. "Because

you had nothing better to do on a Friday night? Or because you were worried that I was going to fall apart?"

"You're not the falling apart type," Paige said, with such conviction Ashley almost believed her.

"Thanks for the vote of confidence."

"Seriously, you've dealt with a lot in the past six months and stood up through it all."

"I had a minor meltdown on Wednesday," she admitted, reaching for her glass. Thankfully the Fedentropin trial didn't prohibit the consumption of alcohol, and the wine she'd drank was already helping smooth the roughest of the edges.

"When you found out Cam had a child? Or when you learned that your sister's pregnant?"

"It was probably a combination of both."

Paige nodded and set a slice of blue cheese on a rye cracker.

"I'm happy for Megan and Gage," she said. "And I'm thrilled about the baby."

"I know you are," Paige agreed.

"I just want to know when it's going to happen for me. When is it going to be my turn?"

"What happened to your appointment at the clinic?"

"I got bumped," she grumbled. "The doctor had some kind of emergency."

Her cousin smiled. "I think that's the nature of the medical field."

"I know. It just seems like one more detour sign on a road that's been littered with them."

"What kind of sign is Cam?"

Ashley sipped from her glass again. "Dead end."

"Are you sure about that?" Paige asked. "Because if I'm not mistaken, that's him walking up your driveway."

Ashley set down her glass before she spilled the contents all over herself. "Don't you dare leave—"

But Paige was already on her feet, reaching for the tray of snacks. "I'll just go refresh this." She turned and smiled at the uninvited guest who had stepped up onto the porch. "Hello, Cam," she said, then slipped into the house before he could even respond.

Cam glanced at the closed door, then at Ashley. "Did I say something wrong?"

She didn't smile at his attempted humor. "Not yet."

He held up his hands in a gesture of surrender. "I just came over to apologize."

"What, exactly, are you apologizing for?"

"For not telling you that I had a child."

She lifted a shoulder. "You don't owe me any apologies, Cam."

"I didn't mean to blindside you."

"It doesn't matter."

"It does," he insisted. "Maybe I figured you would have heard about Maddie a long time ago, but I shouldn't have counted on that, and I should have given you the courtesy of an explanation."

"No explanation required. You dumped me, met someone else, got married, had a child."

"It wasn't quite that simple."

"I'd say it was exactly that simple."

"I'm not going to apologize for not wanting what you did when I was nineteen," Cam said. "Because any nineteen-year-old who wants to marry his high school sweetheart is either blinded by lust or completely without ambition. I'd apologize for hurting you because I was insensitive jerk, but I've already done that and I'm tired of trekking down the same path."

"Then you can just follow the path right back to your own house," she said coldly.

He shook his head. "That would be the easy way, and I'm not taking the easy way again."

"It's a way out," she said. "And that's all you ever wanted."

"Wrong. I wanted *you,* Ashley. I wanted you a hell of a lot more than I should have at that age, and it terrified me."

"Obviously you got over it."

"You'd think so, wouldn't you? But that's the real bitch of it—because I never did."

"You married another woman. Had a child with another woman." Her voice hitched, and she hated him for it. Hated him for the pain she felt every time she thought about the baby he'd given to someone else.

Cam lowered himself into the chair that Paige had vacated. "I married Danica because I thought we wanted the same things. By the time I realized I was wrong, it was too late. We were married, she was pregnant, and even knowing our marriage was a mistake, I wouldn't wish it away for anything in the world because I got Maddie out of it."

Ashley looked away. "It's ironic, isn't it? All I ever wanted was to get married and have a family, and you ran as far and as fast as you could from me because you weren't ready to make that kind of commitment."

"Twelve years ago, I wasn't ready," he agreed, then smiled wryly. "There are still days that I'm not ready, but Madeline doesn't really give me a choice in the matter."

Ashley didn't smile back, but she did ask, "So how did you end up with custody?"

Cam realized he should have been prepared for the question; Ashley certainly wasn't the first person to ask it. Because although the courts no longer awarded custody to mothers as a matter of course and shared custody arrangements were increasingly popular, it was still somewhat unusual for a father to be granted primary care of a child.

He'd always felt awkward explaining the situation, and he'd resented having to make excuses for what he'd believed for so long was simply his ex-wife's disinterest. He knew differently now, but he still didn't know how to make anyone else understand without sharing secrets that weren't his to share.

"Staying with me offered Madeline more stability," he finally responded to Ashley's question. "Especially since Danica was already planning to move to London."

Ashley frowned as she sipped her wine. "And she was okay with that arrangement? She just moved to another continent and left her child behind?"

"We agreed it was best for Maddie."

"Does Maddie see her very often?"

"Not as often, or as consistently, as I'd like," he admitted. "But she did spend the last month of her summer vacation in London with her."

"So why didn't you mention your daughter to me the night you came over here?"

"You mean the night I kissed you?"

"I mean the night you brought pizza," she clarified, as if the kiss was irrelevant.

But he could tell by the color that infused her cheeks that it wasn't irrelevant at all, and that she remembered that kiss as clearly as he did. And as much as he wanted to kiss her again, to prove that the attraction between them was still very relevant, his real purpose in coming here tonight had been to clear the air, not to cloud it further.

"I should have," he finally admitted. "But I don't talk about Maddie very much when she's gone. Not to anyone."

"Why not?"

"Because talking about her makes me miss her even more."

She seemed startled by his response, but then she nodded. "I guess I can understand that."

"She's the center of my world, the reason for everything I do."

"She's a lucky girl." Ashley's voice had softened, taken on

an almost wistful quality. "To have a father so committed to her best interests."

"Does that mean you forgive me?" he dared to ask.

"It means I like your daughter—she's a great kid."

"Her dad's a pretty good guy, too."

"I'm reserving judgment on that," she said, but the smile that curved her lips gave him hope.

Chapter Six

Over the next few weeks, Ashley crossed paths with Cam on a fairly regular basis. He came to school every Wednesday to pick up Maddie and when he did, he usually dropped in to the classroom to chat with Ashley and check on his daughter's progress. The awkwardness between them was fading and Ashley began to think that one day they might even be friends again.

And if Cam sometimes flirted with her, or dropped little hints that he wanted more from her than friendship, she didn't take him too seriously. She didn't dare.

She still thought about the kiss they'd shared in her kitchen, and she still got all hot and tingly when she did, but she had clearly established the boundaries for their relationship and she was determined to uphold them. But she was glad that her appointment at the clinic had been rescheduled. Even if it was still a few weeks away, it gave her something to look forward to and focus on. Maybe when she was finally expecting a baby of her own she would stop wishing she could be the mother Maddie needed so badly and the wife that shared Cam's bed every night.

Because as often as she reminded herself that there could be no future for her with Cam, she nevertheless found herself day-dreaming about the possibility. And as much as she'd always dreamed of having a child of her own, she knew that loving Cameron's little girl would fill the aching void in her heart.

But Maddie had a mother, and Ashley knew that letting her imagination create happily-ever-after scenarios would only end up causing more heartache for herself in the end. She knew it, and yet, when Cam came out of his house as she was walking past on her way home from the neighborhood market Saturday morning, she couldn't deny that her heart started to pound just a little bit faster.

"What perfect timing," he said by way of greeting.

"For?" she prompted cautiously.

"Apparently you mentioned to your class that you like to hike at Eagle Point Park," he said. "So Maddie suggested, as we're heading up there for a picnic today, that we should ask you to go with us."

"It was sweet of her to think of me, but I'm not sure that would be a good idea," she said, far more tempted than she ought to be by the prospect of an outing with Cam and his daughter.

"Why not?"

"I just don't think we should spend too much time together."

"Why not?" he asked again.

"Because," she said, unwilling to admit that wanting to say yes was proof enough to her that it was a bad idea. Because giving in to what she wanted where Cameron Turcotte was concerned had always gotten her into trouble.

"That's hardly a reasonable response," he chided.

"I'm sure it's one you use all the time with your daughter when it suits your purposes."

"Actually, I never say no to Madeline unless I can give her a reason for it."

"While I'm sure that chalks up extra parenting points for you, it doesn't change my answer," she said firmly.

But Cam wasn't dissuaded. "Come on, Ash," he said. "It's not as if we can get into too much trouble in the hills with a six-and-a-half-year-old chaperone."

"I'm not worried," she lied.

"No?"

It was more a challenge than a question, as if he was all too aware of the tug-of-war that was going on in her mind—the struggle between what she wanted and what she knew was smart.

"No," she insisted.

"Then why won't you come with us?" he challenged.

"Maybe I have other plans for the day," she hedged, mentally searching for some excuse, any excuse, that sounded less desperate than making a list of 1001 reasons that getting involved with Cameron Turcotte again is a very bad idea—even if that was exactly how she planned to spend her afternoon in order to ensure that she was clear on all of those reasons.

"Do you?"

"As a matter of fact, I was going to—"

She wasn't sure what she intended to say, because just then the front door flew open and Maddie came racing across the lawn.

"We're going to Eagle Point Park," she announced. "And I made samiches and Daddy packed juice and we're going to have a picnic. Are you going to come with us? Please, Miss Ashley. It's going to be so much fun, but it will be even more fun if you come, too."

And that quickly, all of Ashley's resolutions about putting

distance between herself and Cam and his little girl dissolved in the radiance of Maddie's smile.

"I think a picnic sounds wonderful," she said.

Cam never used to be the picnicking type, but there wasn't anything he wouldn't do for his little girl. So when Madeline suggested packing a lunch and taking it up to the park, it seemed like a relatively harmless request. It wasn't until they were putting together the sandwiches that his daughter mentioned Ashley, and he realized that he'd been set up.

Not that he minded, really. After all, spending time with Ashley Roarke was anything but a hardship. But he did worry that his daughter seemed to have become so attached to her teacher, and so quickly.

Part of it, he knew, was her desperate craving of female attention—something that he was simply incapable of giving her. Another part was Ashley's natural warmth and compassion, traits that made her such a great teacher and an easy target for his daughter's affections.

As they walked along one of the simpler trails, Ashley taught Maddie how to identify different kinds of trees by their leaves. She also pointed out various birds and the tracks of squirrels and raccoons and something that was—no, not a bear—probably just a big dog.

It was comfortable and easy, and Cam found himself wishing that they could spend every lazy Saturday afternoon together like this. Just him and his daughter and the woman he…liked?

The automatic mental pause nearly made Cam smile.

Of course, he liked Ashley. They'd been friends for a long time before they'd ever become lovers. They'd had a lot of similar interests, enjoyed the same books, music and movies. They liked the same kind of pizza, would both rather play baseball than watch it on TV, and appreciated walks in the rain.

In fact, Ashley had once been such an integral part of his life that, when he'd ended their relationship before going away to school, he'd lost not just his girlfriend but his best friend. It had been his decision to cut all ties between them, finally and completely, at least until he was finished college, but that didn't make it hurt any less.

He hadn't seen her again before their high school reunion in the spring, hadn't realized until then how much of a hole had been left in his life when he'd cut her out of it. But the worst part of seeing her again was realizing how much she still mattered to him, and learning that she was in love with and engaged to someone else.

He'd recognized that his feelings were more than a little hypocritical, considering that he'd already been married *and* divorced, but he just couldn't imagine her with anyone else. He didn't want to imagine her with anyone else.

Deciding to move back to Pinehurst when he knew she was planning a wedding to another man had been difficult. But in the end, he'd known it was what was best for his daughter. With Danica now living in London, there was no reason he had to stay in Seattle, and every reason to move closer to his family so that Madeline's grandparents could be part of her life.

"Hurry up, Daddy." Maddie's voice called back to him, prompting his feet into motion.

"Sorry," he apologized, when he caught up to them.

"What were you doing back there?" Ashley asked.

He shrugged the pack off of his shoulders, opened the zipper and pulled out the blanket they'd brought to spread out on the ground. "I thought I saw a...an owl."

"An owl?" She lifted her brow.

"Owls are...noc-tur-nal," Maddie said, carefully enunciating the word and looking to her teacher for confirmation. Ashley nodded.

"That means they sleep during the day and come out at night," his daughter informed him.

He shrugged. "Maybe it wasn't an owl."

"Owls eat mice and frogs and birds." She made a face after reciting that fact, as if the idea was as distasteful as eating peas or Brussels sprouts—her least favorite vegetables.

"Speaking of food," Cam said, beginning to unpack their lunch.

"I hope you didn't bring mice and frogs and birds," Ashley said.

Maddie giggled. "No, we made samiches." She took a plate and balanced it on her lap. "What kind of samich do you want, Miss Ashley?"

"What are my choices?"

"Peanut butter, peanut butter and jam, or peanut butter and banana."

Ashley mulled over the options, finally deciding, "Peanut butter and banana."

Cam watched as Maddie carefully selected three pinwheel sandwiches from the plastic container and arranged them in a semicircle on the plate. Then she added two cookies—peanut butter, of course—and a small cluster of green grapes.

"That looks absolutely delicious," Ashley said, accepting the plate.

Maddie beamed in appreciation of her praise, and Cam felt his heart swell. Until he'd started spending time with Maddie and Ashley together, he hadn't realized how much his daughter needed a woman's attention. She missed out on so much not having a mother involved in her life, and though *his* mother tried to spend as much time as possible with her granddaughter, it wasn't the same thing.

Gayle had mentioned—several times in recent years—that he should think about getting married again, that he needed a wife as much as Maddie needed a mother. But even if he'd agreed with her assessment—and he was definitely on the fence about the wife part—none of the women he'd dated had tempted him to think any longer term than the next date. There certainly hadn't been anyone whom he'd wanted to wake up beside every morning for the rest of his life, and there hadn't been anyone who'd ever made his daughter smile as she was smiling at Ashley now.

Not that he was thinking in terms of marriage with Ashley. Definitely not.

And yet, he knew that if there was a woman who could tempt his thoughts in that direction, it was Maddie's first-grade teacher. Yes, Ashley tempted him. But he knew it was going to take some time to figure out if *he* could still tempt *her*.

Tearing his thoughts back to the picnic, he noticed that Maddie had taken a second plate and was loading it up with all of her favorites.

"What about my lunch?" Cam asked, indicating the last empty plate.

"Ladies always get served first," she informed him primly. "And you can get your own."

Ashley's cough sounded more like a laugh, and when he looked at her over his daughter's head, he saw the amusement that danced in her eyes.

Those beautiful, sparkling violet eyes.

The same eyes that had haunted his dreams for years, and that continued to haunt his dreams now.

He held her gaze for a long moment, a moment that spun out between them, until there were no birds chirping in the trees, until there was no wind rustling through the leaves.

Until there was nothing but the two of them.

Until Maddie broke the silence by asking for juice.

Ashley blinked and looked away, and the moment was gone.

* * *

Something had happened between them at Eagle Point Park. Ashley wasn't exactly sure what, except that something had changed. Until that moment, she'd managed to convince herself that the feelings she had for Cameron were only remnants of a long-ago attraction. And maybe there were still remnants of that attraction, but there were also new feelings stirring inside of her. Stronger and deeper feelings that she'd managed to ignore because they were only *her* feelings.

In the space of a heartbeat, with the heat of just one look, Cam decimated that belief. And the realization that there was still a connection between them, a simmering awareness that pulled at both of them, terrified her.

So when Maddie approached her desk at the end of the day on Monday, it was an effort to smile, to pretend that everything was the same. And then the child's question shattered even that illusion.

"Are you dating my daddy?"

The marker Ashley had been using to prepare a math chart for the next day's lesson slipped from her fingers.

She bent to retrieve it, wishing she could pick up an easy answer to the little girl's inquiry at the same time. Instead, she responded with a question of her own. "Why would you ask something like that?"

"Because I told Victoria that we went on a picnic on Saturday and she said that you must be dating my daddy and maybe you would marry him and be my new mommy."

She had worried that agreeing to go on a picnic with Cam and Maddie was a bad idea—she just hadn't known how bad. And the desperate yearning in the little girl's big green eyes nearly broke her heart.

Ashley carefully recapped the marker and set it aside so she could give Maddie her full attention.

"I'm not dating your daddy," she said gently. "But he and I are old friends and you and I are new friends, and friends spend time together."

The light in Maddie's eyes dimmed. "So you're not going to marry him?"

"No." She swallowed. "I'm not going to marry him."

"But if you're friends, you must like him," she insisted, with the unequivocal reasoning of a first grader. "And if you like him, then you should marry him."

"Lots of people like one another without getting married."

Maddie sighed. "But Grandma says that Daddy needs a wife who will make him happy and I need a mother who cares more about me than her career."

Out of the mouths of babes, Ashley thought, and cautiously asked, "She said this to you?"

Maddie shook her head. "She said it to Grandpa, but I could hear them talking."

"Sometimes adults have conversations that they don't mean for children to overhear, and what your grandma said probably wasn't intended to be repeated."

Maddie nodded. "But I think Daddy should get a new wife, too, 'cause then we could be a family."

The crack in Ashley's heart split open a little wider. "That's something only your daddy can decide."

Cam's daughter sighed again. "I need to go now. Grandma will be waiting for me."

"Okay." And because she figured they both needed it, she gave Maddie a quick hug. "I'll see you tomorrow."

Being summoned for a conference with the teacher wasn't quite the same as being called to the principal's office, but

Cam had an uncomfortable feeling in the pit of his stomach just the same when he heard the message from Ashley on his answering machine.

He glanced at the calendar before he called her back. "I have about an hour at seven o'clock tonight while Maddie's at ballet," he said. "Can I buy you a coffee at Bean There Café?"

"That works for me," she agreed, but still gave him no indication what it was she wanted to talk about.

So he worried about it while he cooked spaghetti for dinner, and though he gently tried to elicit details from Maddie about her day at school, his daughter was uncharacteristically close-mouthed, a fact which only increased his apprehension. They loaded the dishwasher together after they'd finished eating, then she washed up and went to get changed for her dance class, but there was no enthusiasm in her step and no sparkle in her eye.

When he got to the café, he noted that Ashley looked almost as apprehensive as he felt.

"What did she do?" he asked without preamble when he brought their drinks—regular black coffee for him, a cinnamon dolce latte for Ashley—to the table.

"She didn't do anything wrong," she hastened to reassure him. "I just thought you should be aware that your daughter is expressing an interest in you finding a new wife."

He exhaled a sigh of relief. "I thought maybe she'd stabbed that annoying Charlie Partridge with her safety scissors."

Her eyes flashed. "I'm glad you think this is funny."

"I don't," he assured her. "But I was envisioning so many worse things that the truth almost seems anticlimactic." He sipped his coffee, considering her revelation. "How did this come up?"

"She asked me—" her gaze slid away from his, her cheeks flushed with color "—if I was going to marry you."

Despite her obvious embarrassment, he couldn't resist teasing her a little. "Did you tell her that I hadn't asked you…yet?"

"Will you stop joking about this?" Ashley demanded, obviously not amused. "She's at an impressionable age and obviously looking for a mother figure."

"I know," he admitted. "I just didn't realize how much until recently."

Ashley sipped her latte.

"You told me she doesn't see her mother on a regular basis," she reminded him gently. "Is there anything you can do to change that?"

"Not likely. Danica comes to visit whenever it's convenient for her, and that's not more than two or three times a year. The four weeks that Maddie spent in London this summer is more time than she usually spends with her mother in a whole year."

And he wasn't entirely sure she'd spent most of that time with her mother, because she'd come home with a new handheld video game system and half a dozen games that Danica had bought to keep her busy while she "finished up some work."

"What about telephone calls?" Ashley prompted.

"Her mother tries to call once a week."

"Tries?"

He sighed. "What do you want me to say, Ash? I knew when I married Danica that she was committed to building her career. I didn't know that she was committed to her career at the expense of all else, but that's the way it is."

"Okay, so maybe she isn't a candidate for mother of the year," Ashley allowed, "but Maddie is her daughter and she needs her mother."

"Danica doesn't see it that way."

It was obvious that Ashley didn't understand. Hell, he wasn't sure he understood, but he'd long ago accepted that Maddie would never have a close relationship with her mother.

"The truth is," he heard himself say, "Danica never wanted to have children."

Ashley stared at him, as if she couldn't believe what he was saying. He could hardly believe he was telling her. But this was Ashley, and if he wanted a second chance with her—and he'd finally accepted that he did—he had to be honest with her, and he had to trust that she would understand.

"I've never admitted this to anyone else—not even my parents—but Madeline wasn't planned," he confided to her. "In fact, Danica wasn't very happy when she realized she was pregnant."

That was an understatement, but he couldn't admit to anyone, even so many years later, that Danica hadn't been happy at all. In fact, she'd been furious. Having apparently managed to put aside the grief of a previous miscarriage, she was too busy building a career to want to have a baby.

Cam had tried to understand. Maybe it wasn't what either of them had envisioned for a marriage that was barely into its sixth month, he'd admitted, but her pregnancy didn't change their plans, it merely accelerated them. Or so he'd believed, until he'd realized that, despite claiming to be pregnant when they married, Danica never really wanted to have children.

He'd been stunned by her attitude—and furious when she'd suggested terminating her pregnancy. She wasn't an unwed teenager, but a married woman and no way in hell was he going to agree to abort their child.

And so was laid the first brick in the wall that built up between them.

"But she fell in love with her baby when she held her in her arms," Ashley guessed, obviously unable to imagine any other possibility.

Which was exactly what Cam had hoped would happen.

But the truth was, Danica only agreed to have the baby so

long as he assumed complete responsibility for their child after the birth. And he'd gone along with her demands, certain that her attitude toward their child would change through the course of her pregnancy. But the distance between them continued to grow along with the baby in her womb.

"She tried to be a good mother," Cam said in defense of his ex-wife, because he wanted to believe it was true. And because, when he realized some hard truths about her own childhood, he knew she'd handled the situation in the way that she believed was best for their child. "But Madeline was a difficult baby and after working fourteen hours at the office, Danica didn't have the patience for a demanding infant."

"She went back to work right after having the baby?"

"Her career meant a lot to her," he said, all too aware that it didn't just sound like a lame excuse, it *was* a lame excuse.

"More than her family?" Ashley demanded incredulously. "And what about your career?"

"I was still finishing my internship."

"And taking care of the baby," she guessed.

"There was a retired woman who lived above us who helped out a lot, but I was happy to do as much as I could between shifts at the hospital."

"That couldn't have been easy."

"It wasn't easy," he agreed. "But I was happy to do it, to be the one who was there when she cut her first tooth, when she spoke her first word, when she took her first step." And each one of those precious moments was indelibly imprinted on his memory.

"I know I've said it before, but Madeline's lucky to have a dad like you," Ashley told him.

"And a teacher like you," he said.

She finished her latte. "I just thought you should know what was going through her mind."

"I'm a little surprised," he admitted. "She's never mentioned the possibility of me finding a new wife before."

"It might be a factor of her age," Ashley suggested. "She's making friends at school, and they talk about their mothers—it's not surprising that she might look for someone to fill that role for her."

"And that she would gravitate toward you." He reached across the table, touched her hand. "When I came back for the reunion, I was surprised to find that you weren't already married with the half a dozen kids you always wanted."

She pulled her hand away. "Life doesn't always turn out the way we plan."

A truth of which he was all too aware. And yet, coming back to Pinehurst had helped him to see beyond the boundaries imposed by the choices he'd made to the opportunities that might still be found.

"Do you believe in second chances?" he asked cautiously.

She was silent for a minute, and when she finally spoke, it was only to say, "I believe that Maddie's class will be finishing soon, and I need to get home."

Cam pushed back his chair to walk her out.

"Thanks—for the update."

She just nodded.

He watched her go, wondering why she'd refused to answer his question.

Because she didn't believe in second chances?

Or because she did?

Chapter Seven

The Fall Festival was an old but ever-evolving Pinehurst tradition. What had started as a single-day celebration of the harvest back in 1859, when most of the town's residents were farmers, had become a four-day mid-October event.

For Ashley and Paige, it was an annual ritual that brought back mostly fond memories of their teenage years. Because she'd been a bookworm rather than a social butterfly, Megan's memories weren't quite so fond, but they usually dragged her along to the fair with them anyway. And while Megan had critically assessed the engineering of the midway rides, Ashley and Paige were never deterred by her negative attitude.

They would save up their allowance for weeks in advance of the fair, happily giving up their hard-earned cash for a bird's-eye view of the grounds from the top of the Ferris wheel, the thrill of a spin around the Zipper or the heart-pounding fear of the haunted house.

Of course, the fair was more than just the rides and caramel apples and cotton candy. It included a livestock exhibition and agricultural displays with the fattest pig, prettiest flowers and biggest pumpkins proudly displayed with their award-winning ribbons. There were also cooking contests, with local chefs putting their pies and cookies and breads to the test of the judges, and offering samples and selling their wares to the public.

As Ashley walked along the well-trodden dirt path munching on a bag of fresh kettle corn, she had to admit that, at almost thirty years of age, she enjoyed the annual festival probably even more now than she had as a teen. She no longer stood in line for the Zipper, but she'd learned to appreciate the arts and crafts displays more, and she always bought a couple of jars of Mrs. Kurchik's homemade peach jam, winner of the blue ribbon every year for as far back as she could remember.

"You've got to see the baby pigs," Ashley told Paige, steering her cousin toward the barn. Having brought her class on a field trip the previous day, she'd scoped out most of the grounds already.

"It stinks in the barn," Paige protested.

"It smells like animals," Ashley allowed, breathing in the scent of damp earth and fresh straw with just an underlying hint of manure.

Paige wrinkled her nose but gamely followed her through the wide doors. "It smells exactly as it did fifteen years ago."

"Really?" Ashley was surprised by the comment. "We hardly ever came to see the animals when were in high school."

"I wasn't in here to see the animals."

Ashley glanced over her shoulder, saw her cousin smiling.

"Do you remember Marvin Tedeschi?" Paige asked.

She scrambled through her memories to put a face to the name. "Mr. Archer's history class?"

Paige smiled and nodded. "He got to second base with me, right here in this barn during the Fall Festival when we were in tenth grade."

"You went to second base with Marvin Tedeschi?" Ashley stared at her. "The quiet kid with shaggy blond hair?"

"That quiet kid had the lips of a poet and the hands of an artist."

"How did I not know this?"

"You were too busy lusting after Cam Turcotte to notice what was going on with anyone else," Paige said.

Ashley couldn't deny that was probably true, so she only asked, "And what happened after second base?"

Her cousin sighed. "Nothing."

"Nothing?"

"Well, he got to second base a couple more times after that, but we never took it any further." Her lips curved, her eyes glinted. "At least, not until I saw him at the reunion in the spring."

"You hooked up with him that night?"

"I was feeling a little…nostalgic."

"And he was feeling a little…Wilder?" Ashley teased.

Paige grinned. "I'd say he was feeling a *lot* Wilder. And left me feeling very grateful."

"So that was it? You had great sex, then just went your separate ways?"

"Neither of us wanted anything more than that."

"I don't know that I could ever be so casual about intimacy," Ashley admitted.

"Because you don't think about sex for the purpose of physical release but as an assessment tool in your search for a potential husband," her cousin pointed out.

"That's not true."

"It wasn't a criticism," Paige assured her.

Ashley frowned. "It's still not true."

"Have you ever had sex with a guy just because you thought it would be fun?"

Because she hadn't, she only said, "That doesn't prove anything."

"It proves that you're looking for a mate for life," Paige insisted. "And there's nothing wrong with that."

"I'm not looking for a mate at all, not anymore," Ashley reminded her.

"Then you should try sex just for fun," her cousin advised.

She shook her head. "I think I'll keep my expectations low, at least that way I won't be disappointed."

Paige stopped in mid-stride and turned to face her. "I can't believe it."

"What?"

"CBB wasn't even good in bed."

Ashley felt her cheeks flame as she reached out to rub the cow's head. The big, dark eyes closed and the animal seemed to sigh with pleasure. "Sex was...fine."

Paige lifted her brows. "Fine?"

"Look, if it's okay with you, I'd really rather not discuss this now." There wasn't anything she couldn't talk to her cousin about, but if they were going to perform a postmortem on her sex life, she wanted it to be in the privacy of her own home with a glass of wine in her hand, not in a public venue where anyone could overhear their conversation. Not that there were many other people in the barn, but still.

Unfortunately, Paige wouldn't be deterred. "I need to understand this."

"What's to understand?"

"You were going to marry him."

"And?" she prompted.

"And I can't fathom why you would want to marry a guy who didn't rock your world," her cousin told her.

"Maybe my world isn't capable of being rocked," Ashley said, aware that she sounded more than a little defensive.

"Are you saying…never?"

She looked away. "Never with Trevor."

"Sounds like a really bad slogan," Paige said. "Maybe you should suggest he put it on his business cards, as a warning to other unsuspecting women."

Ashley felt her lips curve, grateful that her cousin could make her see the light side of such a humiliating admission. "I'm happy just to move on," she said, doing so towards the pigpen.

"But—oh." Whatever else Paige was about to say was forgotten when she caught sight of the seven piglets, their round pink butts wiggling as they scrambled for position while nursing at their mother's belly. "Oh, they are so cute."

"My kids went crazy, oohing and aahing when they saw them yesterday," Ashley told her.

"Kind of like I just did?"

"Just like that," she agreed.

"Seven babies," Paige mused. "Can you imagine?"

Ashley would happily settle for one baby of her own. At least one at a time. But she pushed the pang of longing aside, as she'd been doing for months now, since the end of her engagement to Trevor and the realization that her dreams of motherhood were slipping further and further away from her.

"Mama Pig doesn't seem to be fazed," she said instead.

"That's because seven is actually a fairly small litter for a pig," a male voice informed her from over their shoulders.

A familiar voice that had Ashley's heart pounding too hard and too fast before she even turned around and confirmed the identity of the speaker. And when she saw Cam, her heart started to pound even harder and faster. He had his daughter with him, and obviously the little girl's infatuation with the piglets she'd seen on her field trip had compelled her to bring her father back to the barn.

"Someone's been doing his homework," Paige noted. "Trying to impress the teacher?"

Cam just grinned.

"Mother pigs can have between eight and twelve babies," Madeline said. Apparently she'd done the homework along with her father and wasn't going to be outdone by him. Then the little girl smiled at Ashley. "I had so much fun visiting the pigs yesterday that I brung Daddy back to see them."

"Brought," both Ashley and Cam corrected automatically.

"Sorry," Ashley said. "The teacher instincts don't clock out after hours."

"No need to apologize," Cam assured her.

From over her shoulder, Ashley registered the sound of a throat clearing. She sighed and turned.

"This is my cousin, Paige," she said to Maddie. "I brought her to see the pigs, too." Then, to Paige, "You know Cam, of course. And this is his daughter, Madeline."

Paige offered her hand to the girl. "It's a pleasure to meet you, Madeline."

Madeline took Paige's hand and shook it awkwardly. "Okay."

"She's six," Cam said, as an explanation of his daughter's response.

"She's adorable," Paige said, and he smiled like the proud father that he was, while Ashley tried to ignore the ache she felt whenever she looked at his little girl and the much stronger sizzle of attraction she experienced whenever he was near.

"There's cows, too, Daddy," Maddie said, tugging on his hand.

"Cows?" Paige interjected, as if they hadn't already come from that direction. "Can you show me where?"

Madeline looked to her father for permission. He nodded

and released her hand, and she immediately headed off for the bovine stalls, Paige trailing in her wake.

"Not very subtle, is she?" Ashley mused.

"You won't hear me complain about having some time alone with you," Cam assured her.

"We're not exactly alone."

"Close enough," he said, and edged nearer to her.

Too close, she thought, as her heart started to pound just a little bit faster. "Cam."

He ignored the warning in her voice and leaned closer. "You smell much nicer than the pigs."

She couldn't help but smile at that. "I should hope so."

"I like your perfume," he told her. "It's similar to what you wore in high school, but sexier."

"It's the same perfume I wore in high school," she admitted.

"Then it must be that you're even sexier now than you were then."

She swallowed and shifted away from him. "Why are you doing this, Cam?"

"What is it that you think I'm doing?" he asked her.

"Flirting with me."

He smiled. "Maybe to see if you'll flirt back."

"I won't," she said, a reminder to herself as much as a response to him.

"What if I took you for a ride on the Ferris wheel? Would you flirt with me then?"

She shook her head.

"How about a spin on the Zipper?"

"I'd be more likely to throw up on you," she warned.

"You used to love the Zipper."

"I used to love a lot of things."

His eyes locked on hers. "I remember."

The potent sensuality in his gaze had the nerves in her belly quivering and her knees trembling. She tightened her grip on the railing, holding on to the wood as she desperately tried to hold her hormones in check.

"And I can't stop thinking about that kiss we shared in your kitchen," he told her.

"It was just a kiss."

"A kiss that keeps me awake at night."

"A kiss that never should have happened," she said firmly, refusing to admit that the memory of that kiss had the exact same effect on her.

"We were always good together, Ash."

She swallowed. "*Were*—past tense."

"That kiss proves nothing is finished between us."

"I'm not going to get involved with you again, Cam."

He stroked the back of her hand, his fingertips tracing lazy circles over the soft skin. She wanted to snatch her hand away, but to do so would be to admit how much his touch affected her, how much he affected her.

"Because you're still hung up on your ex?" he asked.

"Because I have no interest in repeating the mistakes of the past."

"I made the mistake," he said, "when I said goodbye to you."

She couldn't stand here and listen to him sounding so sincerely contrite. She couldn't look into the fathomless depths of his dark-green eyes and not want to believe what he was saying. Because if she let herself believe he was sorry, that he really did want another chance, well, she just might be foolish enough to give him another chance. And that was something she couldn't let happen. She had an appointment at PARC and plans for her life now, plans that didn't include Cam Turcotte or any other man.

So she turned away and started walking in the direction Paige and Madeline had gone. She knew he would follow, but she also knew that he wouldn't continue whatever game he was playing if there was any danger of his daughter overhearing them.

"We have to run," Paige said, as soon as Ashley caught up with her. "I've got a client emergency and need to head back to the office, but I can drop you at home first, unless—" she looked questioningly at Cam.

"That's fine," Ashley said, wondering if her cousin had fabricated the client emergency in an attempt to drop her in Cam's lap.

At the same time, he said, "I can take Ashley home later."

She shook her head. No way was she going to spend a single moment more than was absolutely necessary with Cam Turcotte. "It's okay. I'm ready to go now."

"If Cam doesn't mind giving you a ride, that would simplify things for me," Paige said. "Since I'm closer to the office if I leave straight from here."

Ashley narrowed her gaze, more convinced than ever that there was no emergency. "Well, I don't want to inconvenience anyone, so I'll take a cab."

"It's not an inconvenience," Cam insisted.

"Great. Thanks," Paige said, then kissed Ashley's cheek, waved to Maddie, who had wandered over to look at the bunnies, and bolted from the barn.

Ashley bit back a sigh of frustration.

Cam smiled, as if he knew as well as she that they'd been played. The difference was, he apparently didn't mind, but Ashley vowed that she would have a serious talk with her cousin the next time she saw her.

"The bunnies are sleeping," Maddie announced to her father, her disappointment obvious.

"It must be past their bedtime," Cam said. "As it's also past yours."

"But I'm not tired," his daughter insisted, though the statement was immediately followed by a wide yawn just as an older couple entered the barn.

Cam's parents, Ashley realized, and wondered if this night could get any more awkward.

She'd spent a lot of time in their home and had grown to know Rob and Gayle Turcotte well while she and Cam were dating. But when Cam ended their relationship and went away to school, their paths had crossed much less frequently, and Ashley still felt awkward whenever they did. Maybe it was her own fault, because she'd loved them almost as much as she'd loved Cam and she'd mistakenly assumed they would be her family someday, too. Losing them, less than two years after her own father had passed away, had devastated her almost as much as being dumped by Cam.

"Looks like we're just on time," Rob said, scooping his granddaughter into his arms and making her giggle.

"I wondered where you two had wandered off to," Cam said to his parents.

"Your mother got waylaid by Ethel Mayer and conned into buying raffle tickets for a blanket we won't win and don't need even if we do," Rob explained.

"It's a quilt, not a blanket," his wife chided. "And a beautiful work of art." Then she smiled at Ashley. "This is a pleasant surprise."

"It's nice to see you again," Ashley said, and hoped she sounded half as sincere as Cam's mother.

Maddie, having been set back on her feet by her grandfather, reached for her grandmother's hand. "Come see the piggies, Grandma."

Gayle glanced at her watch. "Only for a quick minute, then we have to get you home to bed."

"But I'm not tired," Maddie said again.

"But Grandpa is," Gayle replied in a staged whisper. "And you know how cranky he gets if he stays up past his bedtime."

Maddie sighed. "Okay. But we have to see the piggies first."

"We'll see the piggies first," her grandmother promised. Then to the others, "Enjoy the rest of your evening."

"Hey," Cam called, as his daughter started to walk away with her grandparents.

Maddie turned and ran back to him. He squatted down so she could throw her arms around his neck and give him a loud smacking kiss. "Bye, Daddy. Love you."

"Love you, too, baby," he said, and something squeezed tight inside Ashley's heart.

Maddie raced back to her grandparents, turning to wave one last time, then Ashley was alone with Cam again.

Cam watched his daughter until she was out of sight before turning to Ashley. "Looks like it's just you and me now."

"Looks like," she agreed.

It was the first time they'd been alone together since their meeting at the Bean There Café, since she'd told him that his daughter was trying to find him a wife. He'd been thinking about that conversation a lot recently, and thinking that he might not object to getting married again.

Not that he was in any hurry to find himself standing at the altar, but he was no longer adamantly opposed to the possibility. Especially when he considered the potential benefits of making Ashley his bride.

Of course, thinking about marriage—even in the most abstract sense—was a little premature when Ashley was as skittish about being alone with him as the newborn foal was about the strangers hovering around her stall. First, they had to get to know one another all over again, and he would have to thank Paige for giving him this time with her cousin.

"So what do you want to do now?" he asked.

"I think I've had enough for tonight," Ashley said, making her way towards the doors. "So I'll just call a cab and—"

"I promised Paige I would take you home," he interrupted to remind her.

"You were conned by my cousin."

He shrugged. "Either way, there's no reason for you to take a cab when I'm going in the same direction."

"Fine," she relented.

"Are you really that opposed to spending time in my company?"

"I'm not opposed at all," she said. "I'm just not interested."

"You sure didn't kiss me like a woman who was not interested."

She glared at him over her shoulder; he just grinned.

"In fact, you kissed like a woman who enjoys being kissed, and touched and—"

"I was dizzy from the loss of blood," she said.

"You didn't lose that much blood." But he picked up her hand, turned it to the light.

"What are you doing?"

"It's called a follow-up exam."

Ashley was tempted to make some comment about playing doctor, but decided that any kind of sexual innuendo was inherently dangerous around Cam Turcotte. Instead she said, "Dr. Alex already checked it out and said everything's fine."

"It looks like it's healing nicely," he agreed. Then he dipped his head and feathered light kisses along the side of her palm. "How does it feel now?"

She felt all kinds of things she shouldn't be feeling, and none of them had anything to do with the fading scar on her hand. "Fine," she managed.

"No tightness? No pain?"

"No." *Not in my hand.*

He smiled, as if he knew exactly what she was thinking, but all he said was, "Good."

"Eli said you did an exceptional job with the stitches," she admitted. "That I probably won't even have much of a scar."

"You've always had pretty hands. I wanted to make sure they stayed that way." He lowered her hand but, instead of releasing it, linked their fingers together and led her toward the midway.

"The parking lot is the other way."

"I know. The Ferris wheel is this way."

"Aren't you anxious to get home to Maddie?"

"She's spending the night at my parents' house," he told her.

"Oh."

"Ferris wheel?" he prompted again.

She glanced up at the towering wheel, felt a quick jolt of excitement low in her belly, though she wasn't sure if it was anticipation of the ride or just the excitement of being with Cam. She decided not to question but to go with her instincts.

"The Ferris wheel sounds like fun," she agreed.

He must have purchased tickets earlier, because he pulled two out of his pocket and handed them to the attendant, and they joined the queue. There were only a few people ahead of them—most of the younger crowd preferred rides that offered more thrill—and it only took a few minutes before they were ushered into their car.

As she slid across the seat to make room for Cam, she thought it seemed smaller than she remembered. Or maybe it was that Cam seemed bigger. Or maybe it was just that her entire body was sizzling with awareness. Whatever the reason, Ashley found herself thinking that she should have nixed his suggestion. But the attendant had already secured the door and the wheel had shifted to load the next car.

They were only about halfway to the top, slowly making

their way round as the cars continued to load, but Ashley felt her tummy drop as she looked down at the crowds below. "I never used to be afraid of heights."

"Are you now?"

"I'm not sure," she admitted, but thought it probably wasn't the height so much as the possibility of falling and found herself wondering about maintenance schedules and metal fatigue and other things she'd never considered before. "Do you think this is the same Ferris wheel we used to ride as kids?"

"It might be," he teased. "Why—are you worried that the old wheel should be retired?"

"Maybe."

He chuckled and slid his arm across the back of the seat. "Do you remember how we used to ride it over and over again?"

She nodded.

"The first time I ever kissed you was at the very top."

She remembered that, too, and how she'd thought the drop in her belly was the car moving, until she realized it hadn't moved at all. That was the day she'd fallen in love with him.

"I think the local high school boys still lure their girl-friends onto the ride to steal kisses," she told him.

"I'm sure it's not a strategy exclusive to high school kids," he said, curling his arm around her shoulders.

She eyed him warily. "Don't get any ideas."

"Too late," he said, just before his lips touched hers.

Chapter Eight

She couldn't pull back—there was nowhere to go. She could have pushed him away—but she didn't want to.

His fingers sifted through her hair, cupping the back of her head, changing the angle of the kiss.

Her eyes drifted shut, her lips parted.

His tongue touched hers, lightly, teasingly.

Her stomach dropped, and this time she knew it had nothing to do with the ride and everything to do with the man.

When she was fifteen, she'd thought Cam Turcotte was a great kisser. Of course, her experience at the time had been extremely limited and Cam's technique had definitely been superior to that of any of the other three boys she'd kissed.

They'd both moved on since then, and though Ashley secretly hoped to find something to criticize so she could stop wanting him so damn much, she couldn't deny that his mastery was confirmed. Somehow he just knew how to do everything right. When to advance, when to tease, when to push, when to withdraw.

His lips were soft but firm, his taste both familiar and different, and altogether too tempting. It would be so easy to sink back into his arms, to pretend that the past twelve years had never happened. But no—she wouldn't let herself fall into that trap again. She wouldn't let herself forget anything of their past or delude herself into thinking they could have a future. She was just going to enjoy the moment for what it was.

When he finally drew back, they were both out of breath.

"This is crazy," she told him.

"I know," he agreed, and covered her mouth again.

She met him halfway this time, as eager and desperate as he. Maybe it was crazy, but it was safe. As long as she stayed on the Ferris wheel, there was no danger of this leading anywhere she wasn't ready to go.

Okay, so maybe she was more ready than she wanted to admit, but she still had no intention of succumbing to the desire that raged through her system. Then his hands slid beneath the hem of her top, his wide palms skimmed up her sides, over her ribs. His thumbs brushed over the aching peaks of her breasts through the satin fabric of her bra. She moaned, and he nibbled on her bottom lip while his thumbs moved back and forth over her nipples, the rhythmic motion shooting tingles through her whole body.

She arched against him, wanting to be closer, wanting to feel every inch of his body pressed against every inch of hers. But they were already as close as they could get in the narrow, swaying gondola of the rickety old Ferris wheel.

Her conversation with Paige came back to haunt her. It had been a long time since anyone had made her feel this good. Too long. And when Cam eased away because the attendant had started to unload passengers, she was undeniably disappointed that the ride—and this exquisite stolen moment—was over so soon.

Cam took Ashley's hand to help her out of the car. He'd been tempted to give the Ferris wheel attendant his last two tickets so they could stay on the ride, but then he'd had a better idea.

"Where are we going?"

"The haunted house," he said, thrusting the tickets at the bored attendant outside before he pulled Ashley through the strips of heavy black fabric that guarded the entrance.

It was pitch-black inside, illuminated by black lights that made her white T-shirt glow like a beacon. He took a moment to appreciate the curve of her breasts and the tight buds of her nipples before he led her through the narrow corridors and across shifting floorboards to his destination, ignoring the eerie moans and cackling laughs and other ghostly sounds.

"Maddie and I were in here earlier, and we took a wrong turn—" he pivoted, fervently hoping that he'd remembered correctly and was taking the right wrong turn "—and got shut in…here."

She moved ahead of him, and he guessed she took about three steps before bumping into the wall.

"Is this some kind of closet?"

"I don't know," he said. And he didn't care. All that mattered was that it was dark and private and that he needed to touch her.

He stepped up behind her, sliding his hands around to her front, under her shirt, over her breasts.

She moaned. "Cam."

"I need to touch you, Ash."

"I'm not having sex with you," she told him, though the tremor in her voice suggested her might be able to change her mind if he really wanted to.

"I didn't bring you here to have sex with you," he told her, and bent his head to kiss her throat. "I just want to touch you."

"You are touching me."

"All of you," he said, shifting one hand from her breast to her hips, pulling her more snugly against him. Her buttocks were nestled against his groin and there was no way she couldn't know how hard he was for her, how much he wanted her. But for now, he just wanted to pleasure Ashley.

His hand slipped lower, dipping beneath the waistband of her denim skirt. She sucked in a breath but didn't push him away, so he let his fingers dip lower, into the soft curls. She gasped, but shifted her legs apart a little more. He accepted the unspoken invitation, delving deeper into the slick heat. Her breath was coming faster now, quick shallow gasps that warned him she was on the edge. Just touching her had him trembling on the precipice himself, but he gritted his teeth and concentrated on her pleasure.

"Let go." He whispered the words into her ear.

She shook her head, denying what he wanted, what they both wanted. But he wouldn't be denied. He kept touching her, stroking her, kissing her neck, nibbling on her collarbone. He knew that she was close. Close but still fighting.

He turned her around, so that she was facing him, and captured her mouth with his own. He kissed her, hard and deep, and slipped his hand between her legs again. He swallowed her shocked gasps and blissful moans as he drove her harder and faster toward the edge, until he felt her tense and shudder and finally…release.

She trembled and sagged against him, burying her face in his shirt. He held her close, gently sliding his hand up and down her back and feeling just a little bit smug as he waited for her breathing to even out again.

"Well." She cleared her throat. "That was a new experience for me."

He tipped her chin up and brushed his lips against hers again. "A good one, I hope."

She sighed. "Oh. Yeah."

Though his own body was still aching with arousal, he managed to grin at the lazy satisfaction in her tone. "Imagine what we might accomplish if we ever found ourselves near a bed," he mused.

She pulled away from him, just a little, but the slight withdrawal was enough to make him realize he should have kept that tantalizing thought inside his head. Ashley had made it clear that she didn't want to get involved with him and what had just happened obviously hadn't changed her mind in that regard.

"As…interesting…as this was, it was a mistake," she told him. "And one I'm not going to compound by sleeping with you."

"It didn't feel like a mistake when you were trembling in my arms. It felt incredible. And right."

"Cam—"

Whatever she was going to say, he didn't want to hear it, so he opened the door and stepped back into the main corridor of the haunted house, where the noise and the dark made conversation impossible.

Because her knees were still shaking and her head was still spinning, Ashley took the hand Cam offered to her and followed him into the darkness. She knew they should talk about what had just happened, but she honestly didn't know what to say, how to explain her own outrageously reckless behavior.

She wondered if her conversation with Paige had lessened

her inhibitions, or if Cam's kisses had short-circuited her usually rational brain. There had to be some kind of explanation for what she'd just allowed to happen in a public place. The fact that they'd been behind a closed door and completely in the dark failed to lessen the shock she felt with respect to her own actions.

The intensity of her release was unlike anything she'd ever known. Or maybe it was the illicitness of the situation that had intensified the experience. Or maybe it was just that it had been far too long since she'd let herself go so completely.

And yet, her body still ached and yearned, wanting more.

Wanting Cam.

There, she'd admitted it. At least to herself. She wanted Cam Turcotte as much now as she'd wanted him when she was in high school. But she was an adult now, a grown woman, not an idealistic girl. A woman who had experienced love and heart-break and who wasn't prepared to walk down that path again.

Paige had been right about the fact that Ashley didn't have sex for fun, and that was why she couldn't succumb to the desire that was coursing through her body. She didn't dare. Because she knew she would never be able to share her body with Cam without letting him into her heart, and she absolutely was not going to fall in love with him again.

No, she had plans for her life, and Cam Turcotte didn't fit anywhere in those plans.

He didn't say anything more as he led her across the still-crowded parking lot to his car. It obviously wasn't as late as she'd thought, but she was more than ready to head home, to say good-night and goodbye to Cam and crawl into bed alone.

Liar.

She scowled at the mocking voice inside her head.

Okay, so what she really wanted was to drag Cam into the

house with her and jump him. Because while her body was still humming with pleasure, she didn't feel completely fulfilled. She wanted him inside of her, moving with her, stoking the long-dormant fire that was suddenly roaring through her body.

I'm not having sex with you, she'd said, and she'd meant those words when she said them. Now, however, she wasn't feeling quite so adamant. Or maybe she was just feeling a little guilty that he had taken care of her needs and she'd done nothing for him.

Of course, he hadn't asked for or demanded anything from her. He never had. The first time they'd ever made love had been on her initiative and, even then, even when he'd had more enthusiasm than finesse, he'd tried to ensure she got some pleasure out of the experience.

While sex had never been an earth-shattering experience for her as a teenager, she'd loved Cam wholeheartedly and un-ashamedly and she'd enjoyed the closeness of being with him. It was a long time after he left before she'd dated anyone else, and longer still before she'd been willing to open up her heart again. But she'd never loved anyone else with the same unrestrained passion; she'd never loved anyone else as much as she'd loved Cam.

And that was precisely why getting involved with him again was a very bad idea.

He pulled into her driveway and cut the engine.

She wanted to protest that he didn't need to walk her to the door, but she knew he wouldn't listen. And maybe she needed to say good-night to him on the doorstep, to prove to herself that she was capable of sending him away even when she wanted to drag him inside.

He came around to her side and walked beside her up to the porch.

"You forgot to leave a light on," he noted.

"I do it all the time," she admitted, sliding her key into the lock. "Unless it's dark when I leave, I don't think about it."

"Then you should have sensor lights that come on automatically when you move in front of them."

She pushed the door open and hit the switch on the inside wall, spilling light onto the porch. "I'm a big girl, and this is a safe neighborhood."

"You're a single woman living alone. There's no harm in being cautious."

"I am cautious," she told him, then proved it by slipping inside before she could renege on her promise to herself that she wasn't going to invite him to come in.

"Lock the door," she heard him call from the other side.

She slid the deadbolt into place, and watched through the sidelight as he walked back to his car and drove away.

Cam slept like hell.

Or maybe it was more accurate to say that he didn't sleep at all. And when he finally caught a glimpse of the sun beginning to peek over the horizon, he gave up even pretending.

It was his own fault, he knew that. Just as he knew that he could take care of the ache in his body easily enough. But he also knew that any satisfaction would be both temporary and superficial. He wanted more than a physical release—he wanted Ashley. He wanted her naked body beneath him, her soft breasts pressed against his chest, her long legs wrapped around his hips—

He shoved the image out of his mind as he pushed back the tangled covers.

He needed a shower. A very cold shower.

And then he needed a plan.

Because he knew better than to think he'd made any

progress with Ashley last night. Sure, it might have seemed like they were on the same wavelength while they were in the haunted house, but he knew that she would do some serious backtracking in the light of day. Hell, she'd started backtracking even before they got in his car to drive home.

He firmly believed that the sizzling sexual attraction between them was proof that the chemistry had never died, but he knew that she still needed some convincing.

He turned off the shower and yanked a towel from the bar. It was early yet, but he would grab a cup of coffee on the way to his parents' house to pick up Maddie—maybe get there in time for some of his mother's buttermilk pancakes—then take his daughter to her ballet class and, afterward, for a quick trip to the hardware store.

Ashley was working at the computer late Saturday morning when the doorbell rang. She was tempted to ignore the summons. She wasn't expecting any company and, as a result of having gotten very little sleep the night before, she wasn't in the mood to chat with anyone selling anything.

But the bell rang again, as if whoever was on the other side knew she was home, so she finally pushed away from the desk.

Peeking through the sidelight and finding Cam on her porch only made her more wary. After what had happened between them the night before, she needed some time to figure out how to deal with him, and how to deal with her own mixed-up feelings.

How the heck was she supposed to carry on a conversation with the man who had taken her to heights of pleasure she hadn't experienced in a very long time? Especially when her hormones were already revving in anticipation of a return trip.

She wanted to pretend that last night had never happened,

but the heat in his eyes as they slowly skimmed over every inch of her body made that impossible.

"What are you doing here?" she asked.

"I need access to your electrical panel."

She lifted a brow. "That's one I haven't heard before."

He grinned. "It's not a secret male code, just a precaution to ensure that I don't get electrocuted while installing your new lights."

"I don't need new lights. And I thought you were a doctor, not a handyman."

"Actually, I'm a doctor who happens to be very handy," he told her. "And I picked up some motion sensor lights for you at the hardware store this morning."

"I don't mean to sound ungrateful," she said, all too aware that was precisely how she sounded, "but I didn't ask you to pick up any lights for me."

"I didn't do it for you, I did it for me."

She folded her arms across her chest. "How does putting up new lights for me benefit you?"

"It will ensure I worry less about you coming home after dark."

"There's no reason for you to worry," she insisted.

"I'm sure that's true, but I'll worry, anyway. So letting me put up these lights would be doing me a big favor."

"That is the most ridiculous argument I've ever heard."

"But creative."

Her lips curved. "I'll give you that."

"So—" he prompted. "Your electrical panel?"

"It's in the basement." She stepped away from the door so that he could enter.

"Was I interrupting something?" he asked, gesturing to the computer desk and the pile of notes she'd printed.

"Just lesson planning. We're studying the growth cycle of

the pumpkin this week in preparation for Halloween at the end of the month, and I was hoping to find some kind of art project that would reinforce the lesson for the kids."

"Don't you just teach the same stuff year after year?"

"I have to cover the same basic curriculum," she admitted, leading him down into the basement. "But I like to implement some new projects or approach the topics from different angles to keep the subjects fresh and interesting."

"I assume that's fresh and interesting for you, since you don't have the same group of kids for more than one year."

She smiled. "Yes, it's for me. I don't ever want to become one of those teachers who bores her students."

"I don't think there's any danger of that," Cam told her. "Maddie is always talking about school and she's always enthusiastic."

"Where is Maddie today?" she asked.

"She went back to my mom's after her ballet class. Whenever it comes to a choice between the hardware store with Daddy or the toy store with Grandma, she abandons me without a backward glance."

Ashley smiled as she gestured to the electrical panel. "Everything's labeled, so it shouldn't be too difficult to find the breakers you need to shut off."

He opened the panel, scanned the tags, flipped some switches. "That's it?"

"For now," he said, closing the panel door. "They'll need to be turned back on again when I'm done."

She nodded and followed him back up the stairs.

It didn't take long for Cam to install the lights. At least, it seemed to Ashley that not very much time had passed before he was back at the door to turn the breaker on again. She was making herself a sandwich and though she still thought it was smart to keep her distance from Cam, it seemed impolite not to offer him some lunch in exchange for the lights.

But if she felt awkward inviting him to stay for a sandwich, it was nothing compared to the discomfort she felt when he picked up the clinic brochure she'd inadvertently left on the counter.

She was dishing up potato salad alongside the sandwiches when she saw him reach for the pamphlet, the bold letters practically jumping off of the front: **PINEHURST ASSISTED REPRODUCTION CLINIC**

Cam looked at the cover, where the date and time of an appointment were noted, then at Ashley. She'd told him about the endometriosis and her participation in the clinical trial, so he didn't understand why she would have an appointment at PARC. Unless—

"Are you pregnant?" he asked her.

Her cheeks flushed and she snatched the pamphlet from his hand. "No."

He hadn't realized he was holding his breath in anticipation of her response until the air whooshed out of his lungs again.

Not pregnant.

That was good, because pregnant was definitely more of a complication than he was ready to handle at the beginning of a relationship—assuming that he and Ashley were at the beginning stages of a relationship. But if she wasn't pregnant—

"Then why do you have an appointment at PARC?"

"I'm keeping my options open."

"Options," he echoed, still uncomprehending.

"I want to have a baby, a family," she said, as if that should have been obvious. "I thought I was on track with Trevor, but obviously that train got derailed. Now I'm looking at some alternatives."

"Don't you think this…alternative…is a little extreme? You're only twenty-nine—"

"And I have endometriosis," she reminded him. "Before I started the drug trial, my specialist recommended radical surgery."

"A complete hysterectomy," he guessed.

She nodded, tears filling her eyes. For a woman who loved children as much as Ashley, that course of action would be devastating.

"Is the Fedentropin helping?" he asked her.

"It's bought me time, but it's not a cure."

Which he knew, of course. After she'd first mentioned the drug to him, he'd done some research. Because the drug was still in the trial phase, a lot of information was restricted, but he had learned that the medication was targeted specifically at women for whom more traditional treatments—usually birth control pills—were unsuccessful.

"But having a baby without a father—"

"Don't lecture me on the difficulties of being a single parent," she warned him.

"I wasn't going to lecture," he denied. "I was just going to suggest that you reconsider all of your options before you pursue artificial methods of conception."

"I have considered all of my options and I'm not rushing into anything. I'm only going to the clinic to get the information I need before making any final decision." She nudged his plate closer. "Now eat."

"You're always so gracious when we sit down at a table together."

"Must be your innate charm that brings out the best in me."

He picked up his fork and speared a chunk of potato. Ashley took a bite of her sandwich, clearly signaling that the conversation was at an end.

But Cam couldn't stop thinking about what she'd revealed. He wasn't surprised that she wanted a child, but he did wonder how far she was willing to go to get what she wanted—and if she was considering that another one of her options might be to find a ready-made family in need of a mother.

He munched on his sandwich and wondered if he'd completely misread the situation with her. Had he made a mistake in believing that he and Ashley were rekindling their romance? Was it possible that she didn't have any interest in a relationship with him and only wanted to be a mother to a little girl who desperately needed one?

It would be the irony of all ironies. The woman he'd married didn't want to have anything to do with her child, and now he was halfway in love with a woman who might only want to be with him because of his daughter.

Chapter Nine

Ashley always looked forward to Sunday brunch with her sister and her cousin. For the past several years, they'd met once a month at Michelynne's Café in the village to eat and chat and have what they fondly referred to as their girl time. Ashley had worried, after Megan and Gage got married, that her sister might start to skip out on their ritual gathering, but she was pleased that the tradition continued to endure.

Sometimes they celebrated, sometimes they commiserated, but always they supported one another unconditionally. So when Ashley announced that her appointment at the clinic hadn't gone quite as she'd hoped, that the doctor she'd met with had insisted she wait six months before pursuing intrauterine insemination, she was surprised by their responses.

"Six months doesn't seem unreasonable," Paige said.

"Six months is half a year—and two-thirds the term of a normal pregnancy," Ashley felt compelled to point out.

"But you're young," Megan said.

"I'm almost thirty," she said, and the knowledge of that birthday on the horizon taunted her. She'd had a plan for her life, and she'd expected to be a wife and a mother long before now.

"You just turned twenty-nine," her sister reminded her.

"And a lot of women today don't even think about having babies until they're in their forties," Paige added.

Ashley shook her head. "I don't believe this. I thought you would be on my side."

"We are on your side," her recently impregnated sister insisted.

"We just think you should take some time to be sure that this is what you want, that this isn't an impulse," her cousin added.

"When have I ever done anything impulsive?"

"Letting CBB put a ring on your finger after you'd been dating only a few months was pretty impulsive."

"Okay—so I made one mistake."

"The mistake wasn't yours, it was his," Paige said loyally. "But I still think, if you really want to have a baby, it should be with someone you care about—not a number and a description in a catalog."

"Since there's no one in my life who fits that criteria, I'll go with the catalog."

Megan speared a slice of peach with her fork. "What about Cam?"

"What about Cam?" Paige echoed, obviously intrigued by the possibility.

"I had a doctor's appointment last week," Megan said, "and ran into Cam at the office, and we chatted for a few minutes."

"And?" Paige prompted.

"And I got to thinking that there were still sparks between Cam and Ashley at the reunion, and that it might not take much to fan those sparks into flame."

"I didn't see them at the reunion," Paige admitted. "But I saw the way he was looking at her at the fair. He was making cow eyes at her over the cows."

Megan snickered.

"Yeah," Ashley said. "His feelings were so deep, he fell in love with someone else as soon as he left Pinehurst."

"I don't think that's quite how it happened," Megan chided gently.

Ashley shrugged. "It doesn't matter. Cam and I were over a long time ago."

"If that was true, you wouldn't be so determined to avoid the man who could give you everything you want."

"I don't want anything from Cam Turcotte."

"Then someone should call a doctor, because you obviously no longer have a pulse," Paige said. "And hey—Cam is a doctor, so maybe he can jump-start your heart."

"I'm glad you both find this situation so amusing," Ashley said.

"Only because you're so obviously in denial about your feelings for the man," her sister said.

Ashley picked up her cup and sipped her cappuccino. She'd already said more than she'd ever intended to say on the subject of Cam Turcotte.

"Think about it," Paige urged. "If you let Cam knock you up, at least then you'd know something about the father of your baby."

"Aside from a basic physical description and necessary medical information, I don't want to know anything about the father of my baby. That's why I decided to go through the clinic."

"Except that now you have to wait six months."

Six months seemed like an eternity when she'd wanted a baby for so long already, but she really didn't see that she had any other option.

"I'll bet you could have Cam in your bed in six weeks," Megan said.

"Six days," Paige interjected.

"Except that I don't want Cam in my bed."

"I'm starting to seriously wonder about your pulse," her cousin muttered.

"Because you're not attracted to him anymore?" Megan asked, ignoring Paige's comment. "Or because you *are?*"

Ashley frowned. "That's an odd question."

"Maybe, but I know how your mind works, and I know that, emotionally, you're still reeling from Trevor's betrayal, so the last thing you want is to stir up feelings for someone else."

Apparently Megan did know how Ashley's mind worked, and her sister's insight was more than a little unnerving. "Since when did you become such an expert on the human heart?" she grumbled.

"Since I was lucky enough to fall in love. I never imagined I could feel anything like what I feel for Gage, and I only want the same thing for you."

"I appreciate your concern," Ashley said. "And while there was a time when I wanted exactly what you have with Gage— and when I was engaged to Trevor, I thought I'd found it— I've since realized that not everyone finds his or her soul mate."

"You're certainly not going to find him if you keep closing the doors that are opened to you."

"Even if I was still attracted to Cam—and okay, I do have a pulse—I'm not foolish enough to get involved with a man who's already broken my heart. Besides, he has an ex-wife and a child, and that's more baggage than I'm willing to carry."

"An ex-wife who lives in another country and an absolutely adorable little girl," Megan clarified.

"Exactly how long were you chatting with him?"

Megan looked her in the eyes. "Long enough to figure out that the man still has a thing for my big sister."

Ashley was less concerned about Cam's feelings than her own, and she looked away before Megan could guess that her big sister still had a thing for the sexy doctor, too.

Nearly a week after he'd found out about Ashley's appointment at PARC, Cameron couldn't stop thinking about their conversation. He knew she would be a wonderful mother, so it wasn't her desire to have a child that unnerved him but her willingness to be injected by some anonymous donor in order to make it happen.

As a doctor, he had counseled patients with respect to all kinds of reproductive options. He had never recommended artificial insemination to a single woman under the age of thirty and he didn't understand why Ashley would choose that course.

But the more he thought about it, the more he thought that they each might be able to get what they wanted from the other. Of course, he first had to find a way to convince Ashley of that.

When he went to pick Maddie up from school the following Wednesday, he decided to put his plan into action. Leaving his daughter playing hopscotch with her friends, he dropped in to Ashley's classroom.

"How do you feel about dinner Saturday night?" he asked her.

"Actually, I'm in favor of dinner every night," she said.

"I meant dinner with me," he clarified.

She hesitated. "And Maddie?"

He shook his head. "Just the two of us, maybe somewhere with actual tablecloths and wine and candlelight."

"Sounds like a date," she said cautiously.

"That's the general idea," he agreed.

"And, for all the reasons we discussed weeks ago, not a good one."

"Forget about Maddie for a minute," he told her, even though he wondered if she could. "This is about us and whether or not you want to have dinner with me."

"I want to," she admitted, albeit with apparent reluctance.

"So why don't we discuss all the reasons you think it's a bad idea on Saturday night?"

Her lips curved, just a little, drawing his attention to that temptingly luscious mouth, stirring erotic memories of the kisses they'd recently shared, and churning up desires that were already almost out of control.

"What time are you suggesting that we have this discussion?" she asked.

"How about seven?"

"That could work," she finally agreed.

He took a step backward, determined to make his escape before she changed her mind. "Good. I'll see you then."

Ashley knew that going on a date with Cam was a bad idea. She knew it when he'd asked and when she'd agreed, but the sensible part of her had temporarily been overpowered by the sexually deprived part. Because while she'd been saying "yes, I'll have dinner with you" what she'd really been thinking was "yes, I want to get naked with you."

It was Megan's fault. She was the one who'd planted the idea of having sex with Cam in Ashley's mind. Okay, maybe the idea had already taken root, but both Megan and Paige had nurtured it so that suddenly all Ashley could think about was having sex with Cam. And as she was getting ready for her date, she did so knowing that she was probably going to be getting naked with Cam before the night was over.

She took a leisurely shower, rubbing scented lotion on her

skin when she was done, searching out her sexiest lingerie. The dress was a recent purchase from Chaundra's Boutique. She'd seen it on display in the window and knew she had to buy it, even if she'd wondered if she'd ever have occasion to wear it. As she wriggled into it, she was grateful she'd gone with her instincts because if there was ever a dress made to entice, it was this one that molded to every curve of her body like a lover's hands.

She'd never before set out to seduce a man. The fact that she was doing so now was both exciting and terrifying. The fact that the man was Cam was even more exciting and terrifying.

She gave a lot of thought to setting the scene. She straightened the bottles and pictures on her dresser, but she didn't set candles around the room or program soft music. She wanted cozy, not romantic. Nothing that would give him the impression that having sex was about anything more than sex.

She put fresh sheets on the bed, fluffed the pillows, then sank onto the edge of the mattress and wondered—for about the hundredth time—*can I really go through with this?*

Did she really believe she could have sex with Cam and not want more? And how much more did she want? Was she looking for a relationship with him—or did she want him to father her child?

And how could she explain to him what she wanted when she wasn't even sure herself?

Well, he knew she wanted a baby. But she'd let him believe that she wasn't in any big hurry to get pregnant and that she would be making an appointment at the clinic when she was ready. And, all things considered, that was still probably the best plan.

Except that the more she thought about having Cam's baby, the more she wanted Cam's baby, and that realization gave her pause.

Before she left the bedroom, she automatically pulled open the drawer of her nightstand, checking for the condoms she kept there. Use of birth control was a habit that she'd never disregarded, not even—thank goodness—with her cheating bastard ex-fiancé. Checking that she was prepared was simply another deeply ingrained habit, but one that introduced new doubts and questions.

She didn't think Cam slept around. She certainly hadn't heard any rumors of him being involved with anyone since he'd come back to Pinehurst. On the other hand, the lack of information might just be a testament to his discretion and not his morals. Although she honestly doubted that he'd have either the opportunity or energy for an affair with a young daughter at home.

But regardless of what she wanted to believe, the fact was, she really didn't know Cam any better than any man she might meet in a bar. And there was no way she would invite a stranger back to her home, to her bed, without gleaning some pertinent personal information about him first.

Could she trust that what she believed about Cam was true?

And could she trust that she was strong enough to share her body without giving him more?

When he'd left Pinehurst a dozen years earlier, he'd taken a good chunk of her seventeen-year-old heart and all of her silly, romantic dreams with him. Now that he was back, she knew she was in danger of falling into the same trap, of letting herself hope and yearn for something that could never be.

One of the reasons she'd decided to go the sperm bank route was that she hadn't found herself attracted to any man since she'd ended her engagement. She knew a lot of good-looking men, men with whom she'd flirted and laughed easily in the past. But Trevor's betrayal had cut deep, undermining both her self-confidence and faith in her own judgment.

If the man who'd claimed to love her and want a family with her could cheat on her even before the wedding, how was she ever supposed to trust anyone else? How could she know that the next guy she met and let herself care about wouldn't do exactly the same thing? How could she know that Cam wouldn't?

And the truth was, she didn't know. Except that she did trust Cam because he'd always been brutally honest with her. If he lost interest in her, he would tell her. He would end their relationship before he moved on, and if he broke her heart in the process, at least he wouldn't cheat on her.

She shook her head, pushing those thoughts aside. He wouldn't break her heart—not this time. Because this time, her decision to get involved with him had nothing to do with her heart. She wouldn't let it.

And yet there was a part of her that couldn't help but wonder if it wasn't already too late. If she was planning to bring Cam back here because she did care about him, because the idea of having *his* baby was one that she'd never completely relinquished.

She shook her head, reminding herself that she didn't want anything from Cam Turcotte except a single night of passion. She would never again make the mistake of loving him.

Considering Ashley's less-than-enthusiastic response when he'd invited her on this date, Cam didn't have high expectations when he went to pick her up Saturday night. Still, he figured her agreement, however reluctant, was the first step in the right direction. He knew exactly what he wanted—he'd figured that out even before he'd made the decision to move back to Pinehurst, in the moment that he'd seen her across the room at their high school reunion. He wanted Ashley.

Maybe the realization shouldn't have surprised him. It

seemed that, for as far back as he could remember, he'd wanted Ashley. There was something about her—her sweetness and gentleness and warmth—that made him feel as if he was the luckiest guy in the world when he was with her.

And he'd made the biggest mistake in his life when he'd walked away from her.

He thought about what his mother had told him, and about the role his father's warnings had played in his decision to go away to school, to leave Ashley behind. He didn't doubt his father's advice had been a factor, because he'd always listened to and respected his parents' opinions. But ultimately the final decision had been his, and the biggest factor in that decision had been his own fear that he loved her too much.

He'd been nineteen years old, with his whole life ahead of him. He'd had places he wanted to go, things he wanted to see and do, and Ashley didn't. Sure, she'd had plans for her life, but they were simple plans. Her career ambition was to be a first-grade teacher. Her personal goal was to get married and raise a family in Pinehurst. And when she talked to Cameron about her plans, it was all too easy to envision himself in the role of her husband, the father of her children, and it terrified him.

Knowing how she'd dreamed of a family, it seemed unbelievable to him that she hadn't married and had half a dozen children in the years he'd been gone. Unbelievable and unbelievably lucky for him.

He knew she wasn't ready to jump back into a relationship with him. After the way he'd walked out on her, she was understandably wary. He still wasn't sure if Maddie's obvious need for a mother figure made her even more so, or if his little girl was the only reason she was even giving him the time of day.

He knew she already loved his daughter. The question was, could she love him? Could she forgive the mistakes he'd made in the past and give him another chance?

That she'd agreed to this date tonight gave him hope that maybe she could.

And when she opened the door to greet him, he suddenly found himself hoping for a whole lot more.

He'd always known she was beautiful. The flawless ivory skin, stunning violet eyes and soft, kissable lips meant that she could be wearing ratty old jeans and an oversized shirt with her hair in a ponytail and she'd look beautiful. Tonight, wearing a siren-red dress and mile-high heels and the same scent that never failed to stir his fantasies, she completely took his breath away.

He closed his mouth, because he was seriously afraid he might drool. The sparkle in her eyes and the hint of a smile on her glossy lips warned that she knew exactly the image she presented and that she'd intended to bring him to his knees.

He was already halfway there, more than ready to beg.

The sound of the deadbolt clicking into place as she turned her key in the lock finally registered through the fog that had taken over his brain and propelled him into action. He took her hand and led her to his SUV.

"A friend of mine recommended a new place that recently opened up in downtown Syracuse, if you don't mind the drive."

"I don't mind," she said.

She stepped up onto the running board and slid onto the passenger seat, and as she did, the skirt of her dress slid up a few more tantalizing inches.

She'd always had incredible legs, and in that dress and those shoes, they were shown to full advantage. Long and lean and tanned and bare.

He forced his tongue back into his mouth and closed the door. It was going to be a hell of a long ride to Syracuse— and an uncomfortable one.

"You said you wanted to discuss all the reasons that this

date was a bad idea," he suddenly remembered, thinking that if he was focused on conversation, it would be a lot more difficult to imagine various and creative ways to get her out of that body-hugging dress.

"I changed my mind."

He glanced over at her. "You no longer think this is a bad idea?"

"I'm *sure* it's a bad idea," she told him. "But I've decided to go with it for tonight anyway."

There was something in her tone, something that tempted him to think that she was willing to go with it further than dinner. Or maybe he was letting his own desires influence his interpretation of her words.

One step at a time, he reminded his overly enthusiastic hormones.

She had agreed to a date, which he figured gave him permission to kiss her good night, but he wasn't going to think any further ahead than that.

And first, they had to get through dinner.

The little Italian bistro was both cozy and romantic and, as Cam had promised, there were neatly pressed cloths on the tables, candles flickering and wineglasses waiting to be filled.

The maître d' led them to a table for two tucked away in a corner, presented them with their menus, and wished them "buona sera."

Their waiter appeared almost immediately with a basket of warm bread, a pot of whipped butter and a pitcher of water. He announced the specials of the day—which included chicken, pasta and fish—and recommended wine pairings for each.

Ashley opted for the pasta, Cam chose the chicken and they both decided on wine.

Although the service was prompt, the atmosphere was relaxed and they chatted casually while they ate, first nibbling on the warm bread, then their salads and finally the main courses when they were delivered.

Ashley finished her second glass of wine before her tortellini, but declined Cam's offer of a third. The two glasses were hopefully enough to lessen her inhibitions about getting naked with Cam, but not so much that he would have qualms about taking advantage of a woman in a less-than-sober state.

There were still a few pasta crowns on her plate when she pushed it aside, but she was afraid that she would be testing the seams in her new dress if she finished them.

The busboy immediately whisked away their dinner plates and the waiter followed on his heels to deliver the dessert menu.

Cam opened the small leather folder.

"Amaretto cheesecake, cannoli, gelato, tiramisu." He read through the offerings, trying to tempt her.

She shook her head regretfully. "Not in this dress."

His eyes dropped, skimming over shoulders that were left bare by the halter-style top before dipping lower to follow the plunging neckline to the curve of her breasts. She felt the warmth of his gaze like a caress, and her nipples puckered instinctively. The flare of heat in his eyes warned that her body's response had not gone unnoticed, nor unappreciated.

His eyes shifted to hers again, his lips curved. "Did I mention that I like the dress?"

She swallowed. "Not in so many words."

He leaned closer and dropped his voice. "Did I mention that I'd really like to get you out of that dress?"

"Not in so many words," she said again.

"Do you still think being here with me tonight was a bad idea?" he asked, his voice thick with desire, his eyes dark with promise.

Ashley knew that if she told him yes, if she gave any hint that she regretted the impulse that had led her to accept his invitation, he would back off, he would give her space. But she didn't want space—she wanted Cam.

"I think," she said, keeping her gaze steady on his, "that being here with you might only be the first of several bad ideas we try tonight."

He closed the menu.

The waiter, obviously watching for his cue, immediately appeared. "Dessert, sir?"

Cam shook his head, his eyes never leaving her face. "Just the check, please."

And the tingles that had started low in her belly began to spread to her fingertips and her toes and all the erogenous zones in between.

He took care of the bill then pushed back his chair and offered her his hand. His grip was warm and strong, and Ashley's knees trembled as she thought of those hands moving over her body, touching her, teasing her, pleasing her.

She was so caught up in these erotic thoughts that she didn't even notice the other man until he stepped directly in her path.

"Hello, Ashley."

Her mood plummeted, and she silently cursed her ex-fiancé for killing the mood as she forced a smile to her lips. "Trevor. Hi."

Then Cam's hand squeezed hers, questioning, and the tingles surged through her blood again. And she knew that Trevor couldn't ruin anything else for her—and especially not her plans to be with Cam tonight. So she smiled back at her date, reassuring.

"I just finished dinner with a colleague," Trevor said. "But she had to run, so why don't you and your…friend…join me for coffee?"

If he was hinting for an introduction, he was going to be disappointed. Ashley had no intention of tainting her evening with Cam by bringing him into this confrontation. Instead, she lifted a brow and asked, "Is that the colleague you're currently sleeping with? Or have you made your way through the entire office staff already and moved on?"

Trevor's face flushed. "Really, Ashley, there's no need to be snide."

"I'd say there's every reason, except the truth is, I really don't give a damn who you're screwing anymore."

"I thought—I'd hoped—that we could have a rational discussion about our relationship, but obviously you're still hurting."

He stepped back so she could pass, but Ashley couldn't let him have the last word. "We don't have a relationship and I'm not still hurting, I'm simply over you. Completely."

She started to walk away then, but her hand was still linked with Cam's and he wasn't quite ready to go.

"I wasn't sure I'd ever have the opportunity to meet Ashley's ex-fiancé," Cam said to Trevor. "But I'm glad we saw you here tonight because I really wanted to thank you."

Trevor scowled. "Why are you thanking me?"

"Because you screwed up with the most amazing woman you'll ever know and she's going home with me tonight."

Ashley didn't bother to hide her smile as she and Cam finally exited the restaurant. "I can't believe you said that to him, but it was a great line."

"It was petty and mean, but I couldn't resist."

"It was also wrong," she informed him.

"You're not going home with me tonight?" he guessed, opening the door of his SUV for her.

She heard the disappointment in his voice and felt a surge of purely female satisfaction. Because she knew—despite her blatant invitation in the restaurant—that Cam wouldn't push her for more than she was ready to give. And maybe there was a part of her that was tempted to tease him a little more, but the temptation wasn't nearly as strong as the desire that was churning in her veins.

"No." She leaned in to kiss him, slow and deep. "You're coming home with me."

Chapter Ten

Cam blatantly disregarded the speed limit on the trip back to Pinehurst, anxious to get Ashley home before she changed her mind and reneged on her offer.

"Whose idea was it to go all the way to Syracuse for dinner anyway?" he grumbled, when he finally turned onto Chetwood Street.

Ashley laughed. "It was your idea. And it was a good one. Dinner was fabulous."

"There are good restaurants in Pinehurst."

"Maybe we'll try one of those next time."

He pulled into her driveway, shut off the engine. "Does that mean there's going to be a next time?"

She lifted one shoulder. "That depends on how the rest of the night goes."

He helped her out of the SUV and walked her to the door. "Is that a challenge?"

She turned her key in the lock before pivoting to face him. "Are you up to it?"

He pressed against her, reassuring her that he was very definitely up for the challenge.

Ashley responded by sliding her hands up his chest, linking them behind his head and pulling his mouth down to hers. She teased him with her lips and her tongue, with the fingertips that stroked the back of his neck, with the breasts that rubbed against his chest, until he was tempted to take her right here and now, against her front door, with her skirt hiked up around her hips and her legs locked around him.

The mental image, enticing though it was, forced him to take a step back.

"Give me five minutes," he told her.

She lifted her brows. "I was hoping it would take a little longer than that."

He chuckled. "I'm going to park my car in my own driveway so we don't give the neighbors reason to talk. And then—" he brushed his lips against hers "—we will have all night."

It was a tantalizing promise that made her heart pound and her knees weak, but Ashley wasn't looking for promises. She wasn't looking for anything more than this one night, even if she had slipped and mentioned the possibility of a next time. But more than one date constituted dating, and dating implied a relationship, and Ashley didn't want a relationship. She only wanted to ride the tide of euphoric lust that seemed to wash over her whenever she was with Cam.

The intensity of the desire was both reassuring and unnerving. Reassuring because it had been so long since she'd wanted to be with any man. And unnerving because she'd never wanted any other man as much as she wanted Cam.

When she'd met Trevor, when she'd decided to marry him, it hadn't bothered her that she didn't feel the same feverish excitement she'd felt with Cam. Because she'd attributed the intensity of her feelings for Cam to the hormones of youth and, by the time she met Trevor, she'd grown up. She didn't want or expect to be swept away by desire.

And yet, the most casual brush of Cam's hand against her arm had her feeling that same euphoric anticipation, and just the touch of his lips to hers inspired the same unrestrained eagerness to tear off his clothes and join their bodies together.

She stood at the door, watching for him. Waiting. Wanting.

And then he was there, and she was in his arms.

He flipped the lock as he pressed her back against the door. His mouth descended on hers again, his tongue sliding between her lips, teasing, tempting. She wrapped her arms around his neck, pressed her body closer. Her breasts rubbed against the solid wall of his chest, her nipples pebbling. She shifted her hips, angling them to meet his, and felt the hard press of his erection against the throbbing ache between her thighs. Fireworks erupted inside of her, little bursts of pleasure that left her gasping with shocked delight even as her body ached for more. So much more.

As if in response to her unspoken demand, his hands curled over the curve of her bottom, lifting her off the ground to press her more intimately against him.

Heat rushed through her veins, lust quivered in her belly. She felt hot and willful and reckless, and she didn't care. She only wanted.

Ashley's legs circled around his waist, anchoring her pelvis against his, and Cam realized that it was possible for the human body to go from zero to sixty in point-two seconds. And then she began rocking her hips, and the erotic motion threatened the already tenuous grip that Cam had on his self-control.

"If we don't find a bed soon, it's going to be too late," he warned her.

"Upstairs. First door on the left."

He pushed open the door but didn't bother searching for the lights. He let his instincts—and the thin sliver of moonlight that slanted through the open blinds—guide him.

Her bed was only a double, which might have disappointed any other man who was used to sleeping in a king. But it was Ashley's bedroom and he didn't plan on getting much sleep—two factors that more than made up for the narrowness of the mattress.

He laid her on the bed and sank down with her.

"I can't believe how much I want you," he admitted. "How much I've wanted you since I first saw you again at the reunion."

"I didn't invite you up here for conversation," she told him.

"And I'm grateful for that," he said. "But I can't help but wonder what changed your mind?"

She tugged his shirt out of his pants. "Do you really want to talk about this now?"

"No," he admitted, his breathing more than a little strained. "But something tells me that we should."

Instead, she leaned closer to nibble on his earlobe and whisper a very erotic suggestion to him. And all thought and reason drained out of his head along with the blood that surged quickly south.

He grasped the hem of her skirt and slid it upward, his hands guiding it over the curve of her thighs, her hips, her waist, her breasts. He stopped kissing her only long enough to tug the garment over her head and toss it aside.

He couldn't see much more than shadows, and he wanted to see her, needed to see her. So he reached for the lamp beside the bed and switched it on. Soft light spilled out from beneath the shade, illuminating her. And for the second time that night, just looking at her took his breath away.

He laid her back on the bed and took a moment simply to absorb the sight of her. From the golden hair splayed over the chocolate-brown pillowcase, to the graceful slope of her shoulders, the swell of her breasts covered in sexy black lace, and the indent of her narrow waist. From the subtle flare of her hips to a triangle of matching black lace at the apex of her thighs, and down the long, lean legs to sexy little toes.

She'd been too thin as a teenager, her curves barely existent. She was definitely a woman now, a little softer around the edges, her curves a little fuller, and his desire for her now even stronger.

He eased her over onto her stomach.

"What are you…." The indignant question faded on a sigh as his lips touched the base of her spine. "Oh."

He finished kissing each of the five freckles in turn.

"I had to make sure they were still there," he told her, and rolled her onto her back again.

"I'd forgotten about them," she admitted.

"I couldn't forget them…or you." He touched his lips to hers. "You were—and are—perfect."

Her lips curved, just a little. "And you're still dressed."

He stripped away his shirt and pants and socks, but kept his briefs on for the moment. As he knelt over her on the bed again, he had a sudden, disconcerting thought.

"I wasn't planning for this to happen tonight," he admitted. "And I stopped carrying condoms in my wallet a long time ago."

"I take care of myself," she assured him.

"You're on the Pill?"

He saw a flicker of something in her eyes, then she quickly looked away. Cam wasn't sure what to make of her lack of response, but then she drew his head back down to her.

"Don't worry," she said, and kissed him—long and slow and deep.

He sank down onto the bed with her. She was soft and warm and willing, and he wanted nothing else as much as he wanted to sink into the welcoming heat of her body. His body urged him on, clamoring for release of the tension that had been building for days, weeks, months. A release that only she could give him.

But she deserved better than that. Considering their history, she deserved a lot better. He'd loved her when he was a boy, but he hadn't been careful with her. He'd hurt her, and that was something he'd never wanted to do. And though he knew there was no way to make up for what had been done in the past, he could at least make sure this experience was a good one for her.

So he took his time, touching her slowly, carefully. His fingertips danced gently over her skin, tracing the scalloped cups of her bra, stroking the sides of her torso, the lace edge of her panties, the soft insides of her thighs. Then his lips followed a similar path, lingering here and there, letting her soft sighs and moans guide him.

He unhooked the clasp at her back and slowly pulled her bra off. As the lacy fabric slid across her breasts, over her nipples, her breath caught, her eyes darkened.

"Cam." It wasn't just his name, it was a plea.

"This is the first time we've actually made love in a bed. I don't want to rush it."

"I have no objection to rushing…the first time," she told him.

He chuckled. "I'll bet I can change your mind about that."

"Do you think you could forget about my mind and focus on my body?"

"Believe me, I'm focused," he told her, and dropped his head to take a turgid nipple in his mouth.

She arched instinctively, urging him to take more, to suckle deeper, and moaned when he accepted her invitation.

"Oh…my…oh…Cam."

He moved to the other breast, gave it the same thorough attention until she was squirming and panting.

"Cam, please."

"Tell me what you want."

She didn't hesitate to respond. "You. Inside of me. Please."

He nibbled gently on her bottom lip, teasing. "I don't remember you being quite so impatient."

"I don't remember ever wanting anyone as much as I want you right now," she admitted breathlessly.

It was gratifying to know that she felt the same way he did, but he continued his leisurely exploration, determined to show her how very much he wanted, and how much he wanted to please her.

His lips trailed down her throat, skimmed between her breasts, over her belly. He pushed her panties over her hips, and stripped them away. Then he spread her thighs and continued exploring her body with his mouth.

Ashley sucked in a breath.

"Cam." His name was both a reverent whisper and a heartfelt plea, and he responded.

His tongue dipped and dabbled. Slow, deep strokes alternating with short, rapid flicks that had her mind spinning and her body exploding like a Fourth of July fireworks finale.

She sobbed out his name as her body trembled and shuddered.

Finally he rose over her.

Her body was still quivering with the aftershocks of pleasure, but she suddenly felt cold.

She should have been filled with excitement and anticipation. This was what she'd been waiting for—not just the merging of their bodies but the potential merging of their DNA.

But as much as she wanted a child—as much as she wanted Cameron's child—she knew that going about it this way was wrong. She couldn't do it.

"Wait," she said.

His brows lifted. "*Now* you want me to wait?"

She reached blindly for the handle of the drawer in her nightstand, then fumbled around inside until her fingers found a small square packet.

Cam didn't ask any questions or make any protest. He simply took the packet from her hand, tore it open and quickly sheathed himself, and the icy numbness that had gripped her heart melted away.

"Am I still waiting?" he asked, his voice laced with both amusement and tenderness.

She shook her head and lifted her legs to hook them around his waist again. "No more waiting," she said.

He took her at her word and plunged into her.

She gasped and shuddered and clung to him as he moved inside of her.

She felt the pressure building inside again, a tight, spiraling tension deep in her womb, a sharp, aching need that grew more desperate with each thrust of his hips.

She wanted more.

She wanted everything.

And he gave it to her.

With his hands, his lips, his body, Cam took her to heights of pleasure she had never before experienced, could never even have imagined.

If she'd been able to think, she might have worried that she'd made a very big mistake by inviting Cam to her bed. But there was no thought, no reason. There was only layer upon layer of exquisite sensation, taking her higher and higher, until she flew apart in an explosion of white-hot light.

* * *

Ashley stared up at the ceiling, though she couldn't see anything through the tears that filled her eyes.

Nothing had gone according to plan since he'd shown up at their high school reunion more than six months earlier. Tonight, everything had spun completely out of her control.

"What's wrong?" Cam asked gently.

She shook her head. "It wasn't supposed to be like this."

"I'm a little out of practice," he admitted. "But I didn't think it was so bad."

She managed a smile. "It was supposed to be sex—primal and wild and meaningless."

He brushed his lips against hers.

"We could try again."

He sounded so hopeful she had to laugh, even as she shook her head. "I don't think so."

He kissed her again, and the touch of his mouth was so tender and affectionate she could hardly stand it. He was being so sweet and so kind, and she'd behaved so horribly.

"Tell me why you're crying," he said.

"Because I'm a rotten person."

"I happen to think you're an incredible woman," he told her, kissing her softly again. "Warm, passionate, giving."

She pulled away from him and slipped out of the bed as more tears spilled onto her cheeks. She swiped at them impatiently. "Do you know why I invited you to come back here tonight?"

"Because you were overcome by lust?"

She tugged on her robe, belted it at her waist, and turned to face him. "Because I want to have a baby," she said. "Truthfully, my decision had nothing to do with you aside from the fact that you were willing to get naked with me."

He plumped the pillow and settled back, apparently unconcerned by her revelation.

"Not just willing but eager," he admitted.

"I would have had sex with anyone. You were just convenient."

She'd thought he would be angry, insulted. Maybe she wanted him to be angry and insulted, to push his far-too-sexy body out of her bed, yank on his clothes and storm out of her bedroom and her life forever.

Instead his lips curved, and when he spoke, his words were tinged with amusement. "Do you think so?"

She frowned at him. "Why aren't you furious with me?"

"Maybe because I know you better than you know yourself."

"You don't know me at all anymore," she insisted.

"So tell me," he said, folding his hands behind his head in a casual pose that matched his tone, "why a woman who is desperate to get pregnant would suddenly, at the point of no return, thrust a condom into her partner's hand?"

She didn't know how to respond to that. She wasn't entirely certain she knew what had motivated her actions, whether it was deeply ingrained caution with respect to unprotected sex or an attack of conscience. She only knew that when it came right down to it, she couldn't deliberately deceive him like that.

"Okay, I'll tell you," he said, when she remained silent. "It was because you're *not* a rotten person. Because you're neither deceitful nor manipulative. Because you would never use someone else so callously."

"I almost did," she insisted. "The only reason you're here is because I wanted to trick you into getting me pregnant."

"And if you'd gone through with it but not ended up pregnant? How many times do you think you could trick me? How long do you think you could have continued the charade?"

"As long as I had to."

He caught her hand, tugging her back toward the bed. She let herself be drawn back down onto the edge of the mattress but held herself away from him. "Honey, you couldn't keep up the charade for one night."

"But I want a baby." Her voice hitched and her eyes filled with moisture. "I really do. I even had an appointment at the clinic, but the doctor there insisted that I wait six months."

He shifted slightly so that he was sitting with his arms around her, and his lips brushed away the lone tear that spilled onto her cheek. He didn't say anything for a minute, for several minutes, in fact, but he continued to hold her.

She let herself take comfort from his embrace, because she was sure that once he had a chance to fully absorb what she'd tried to do, he would hate her. And she wouldn't blame him if he did. What she'd almost done was unconscionable and unforgivable.

"It seems to me," he finally said, "that there's a relatively simple way to ensure you get what you want."

It wasn't so much the words as the tone that made her heart skip a beat. She swallowed, hardly daring to let herself hope but needing to ask. "What—" she licked her suddenly dry lips "—what are you suggesting?"

"That maybe we should replay that last scene—but forget about birth control this time."

Chapter Eleven

Ashley stared at him as if she couldn't quite believe what he was saying. Cam could hardly believe it himself. But it seemed to him the obvious solution to give both Ashley and him what they most wanted. She wanted a baby and he wanted her.

Of course, he knew it really wasn't that simple. Ashley wasn't looking for any kind of long-term commitment. The fact that she'd gone so far as to make an appointment at the reproductive clinic proved that she only wanted one thing from any relationship between them—a baby. He, on the other hand, wanted her in his life. Not just for one night, but forever.

So maybe their wants seemed to be at opposite ends of the same spectrum, but Cam believed they would find common ground with a baby.

Yeah, because that worked so well with your ex-wife.

Cam ignored the mocking voice of his conscience because

he knew the two situations were completely different. He hadn't known Danica nearly as long or as well as he knew Ashley, and he was confident that a pregnancy would bring him and Ashley even closer and help break down the barriers that she'd been working so hard to maintain.

"Why?" she finally asked, her voice tinged with both hope and wariness.

"Because that's the only way we'll make a baby."

She swallowed. "I mean, why are you willing to do this?"

"Because I can't imagine anyone who would be a better mother than you," he said. He'd spent enough time with her and Madeline to believe that if there was a woman who was meant to be a mother, it was Ashley. She had a natural warmth that children gravitated toward, and an innate gentleness that encouraged trust and confidence.

"But…what would *you* get out of this arrangement?"

He smiled. "I thought that would be obvious."

"Sex?" she asked skeptically.

"The value of which cannot be overestimated," he assured her. "But more than that, I get to spend time with you."

"I'm not looking for a relationship," she said, confirming his suspicions. "I'm not looking for a husband or even a father for my child."

"Just a not-so-anonymous sperm donor." He unfastened the knot at the front of her robe.

She nodded, though he thought he detected the slightest hesitation first.

Or maybe he was only hoping she hesitated. Just as he was hoping this little experiment of his didn't completely backfire. Because he wanted a lot more than sex from Ashley—he wanted her back in his life. But he knew that she wasn't ready to hear that, so he would play the game according to her rules for now.

He pushed the silky fabric off her shoulders. "And making love with me once or twice or even a dozen times isn't going to change that," he continued, wanting her to know that he understood the boundaries she was determined to set.

"*Having sex* with you a *hundred* times isn't going to change that."

"I got that," he said, and lowered his head to take one rosy nipple in his mouth, suckling hard.

Ashley moaned. "I mean it, Cam."

His tongue circled the moist, turgid peak. "I know you do."

"I just want to be sure there are no misunderstandings."

"None at all." He turned his attention to her other breast, confident that he understood her better than she understood herself. Because he didn't believe that Ashley could share her body without opening her heart, and he was counting on physical intimacy leading to emotional intimacy, and betting with his whole heart.

"Well, then." She sighed, arched. "What are you waiting for?"

He lifted his head to look into those stunning violet eyes.

"You," he said. "It seems as if I've been waiting for you my whole life."

Her brow furrowed. "Cam—"

He captured her mouth, swallowing whatever protest she might have made to the words he'd never intended to say aloud, no matter that they came straight from his heart.

Her lips softened beneath his, and she sank back onto the mattress, pulling him down with her.

His hands moved over her, skimming over the satiny smoothness of her skin, tracing the softness of her curves. His fingertips brushed the damp curls at the apex of her thighs, and she quivered.

"Cam." Not a protest but a plea this time.

He stroked her cleft, sliding two fingers deep into her silky wetness, and slowly withdrawing again. Her breath was coming in short, shallow gasps now, her hips instinctively pumping to match the rhythm of his strokes.

"Let go." He whispered the words against her lips, but she shook her head.

"I want you…inside of me."

It was a request he couldn't refuse.

He straddled her hips and, in one long, deep thrust, buried himself in her slick heat.

She gasped, as spasms immediately began to rock her body; he groaned, and held on while her muscles clenched him like a slippery fist.

They plunged into the abyss together.

Cam awoke the next morning to find Ashley's head tucked into his shoulder and her arm draped across his chest. She'd assured him that having sex wouldn't change anything, but he knew that it already had. Because she hadn't let herself cuddle up to him before she'd fallen asleep, but sometime during the night, her body had instinctively turned to his. He took that as a very good sign.

But for now, he reluctantly eased himself away from her and gathered his scattered clothing to dress. He considered using Ashley's shower but worried that the sound of the water might wake her. And though he wouldn't mind if she woke and decided to join him under the spray, the repercussions of that would definitely put him behind schedule.

But he took the time to put on a pot of coffee, because he desperately needed a hit of caffeine and because he wanted to show Ashley that he could be useful outside of the bedroom, too. When the pot was full, he poured a cup for himself and took a second into the bedroom. He set the cup on the table beside the bed where Ashley was still sleeping, and bent to brush his mouth against hers.

Her eyelids flickered, her lips curved.

"Hey, sleeping beauty."

"What are you doing up so early?" she asked him.

"I'm meeting my parents and Maddie at church," he told her. "It's become something of a Sunday morning tradition since we moved back."

"Oh," she said, but he was sure there was a tinge of disappointment in her tone.

"You could come with me," he suggested, but without much hope.

Her eyes widened. "To church? With your family?"

"Sure," he said, deliberately casual.

She shook her head. "I don't think so."

"You have something against going to church?"

"I'm not opposed to attending church in general," she said. "But with you—yes."

"Because?" he prompted, though he was pretty sure he already knew her answer.

"Because it would give your daughter and your parents and everyone else at Holy Trinity the idea that we're...involved," she told him, confirming his suspicions.

"Because we're not," he said.

"Right," she agreed.

"We're just having sex."

"Right," she said again.

"I'll keep that in mind," he promised, and kissed her again.

He left the house with a coffee cup in his hand, a smile on his face and the conviction that Ashley Roarke was the one who didn't have a clue what was really going on between them. And he figured it was probably a good idea to keep it that way, at least for now.

* * *

Every Wednesday afternoon, Cam left the clinic early so that he could pick Madeline up from school. On those days, he frequently popped in to the classroom to chat for a minute or two with Ashley, and she'd been impressed by the interest he took in his daughter's daily activities. He asked questions not just about her school projects, but about her classroom habits and interactions with other students.

On the Wednesday following the Saturday night he'd spent in her bed, Ashley didn't expect to see Cam because Madeline had happily announced to her that she was going to Victoria's house for a playdate after school. But when she exited the building, she found him waiting for her. Her pulse jolted, then raced, proving she was far more affected by his presence than she wanted to be.

"This is a surprise," she said.

He fell into step beside her. "Since Maddie was having a playdate at Victoria's house, I thought I'd invite you for a playdate at mine."

The invitation had desire churning low in her belly, but she shook her head. "I have some prep to do for the new science unit we're starting tomorrow."

"Do you have to do it now?"

She hesitated.

"Because if you're serious about wanting to have a baby, you should take advantage of opportunities like this."

Of course, she was still serious about wanting a baby, but she was also having serious doubts about the wisdom of enlisting Cam's assistance with her plan. "I'm having second thoughts," she admitted.

"About?" he prompted.

"Using you for my own purposes."

"It's demoralizing, but I think I can stand the humiliation."

The dry tone made her smile. "Or maybe you're just horny."

"That could be a factor," he agreed. "Although it's certainly one that works in your favor."

"I'm just worried that we jumped into this too fast, without clearly thinking it through."

"What's to think about? I want to have sex with you, you want to get pregnant, and having sex is a pretty good way to do it."

Her gaze narrowed. "It sounds perfectly logical and reasonable when you say it like that."

"So what's the problem? Because I thought the sex between us was pretty darn spectacular."

Her cheeks flushed. "Can we not talk about that here and now—where there are impressionable young children walking home from school?"

"None of those impressionable young children are close enough to hear anything we're saying," he assured her. "But if you prefer, we can finish the conversation at my place."

"I'm pretty sure if we went to your place, we wouldn't finish this conversation."

"Your choice," he told her, his tone serious now. "But I have a few hours free and I'd like to spend them with you."

"*That's* the problem," she told him.

He lifted his brows. "Wanting to spend time with you is a problem?"

"Yes," she said, all too aware that her response made her look as foolish as she felt. But she wanted boundaries—she *needed* boundaries. "Because you say things like that and it makes me want to spend time with you, and this—" she gestured between them "—isn't supposed to be about anything but sex."

"My initial offer was for sex," he reminded her.

She huffed out a breath. "Except that it's not that black and white."

"And the gray areas scare you," he guessed, the teasing glint gone from his eyes.

She nodded, though it was his insights that scared her even more and compelled her to remind him, "I'm not looking for a relationship. Not with you. Not with anyone."

"Because you're still getting over a broken heart—"

"Trevor didn't break my heart," she interjected. "He broke my trust."

"And that takes longer to heal," Cam acknowledged.

"But even if I didn't have questions or doubts because of what happened with Trevor, I still wouldn't want a relationship with you," Ashley told him. "Because you *did* break my heart."

"I was young and foolish," he said, and sounded genuinely remorseful.

"We were both young and foolish," she admitted.

"So why can't you forgive me?"

She sighed. "I have forgiven you; I just won't set myself up for the same heartbreak again."

"But we're not the same people we were then," he reminded her.

"No," she agreed. "And that's why you have even more reasons to be wary than I do."

"You're talking about Maddie."

"Of course I'm talking about Maddie. She made the mental leap from a picnic in the park to a potential wedding in less than forty-eight hours. Imagine what she would think if she knew we were actually involved."

"Maybe it's not Maddie's expectations that you're worried about," he said, stopping in front of his house. "Maybe it's your own."

He was right, of course, but that didn't alleviate her concerns. "Maybe it is," she allowed. "And maybe—"

"Maybe we should both stop worrying about what might

or might not happen and just let it happen," he suggested, and touched his mouth to hers.

Even as Ashley responded to his kiss, she knew that was exactly what she was afraid of. That if she just let things happen, she would end up falling for Cam all over again. But she wasn't yet ready to admit that to him, so when he finally eased his lips from hers, she only said, "This 'it' that I should just let happen...are you talking about sex again?"

"It's humiliating how easily you see right through me," he said.

They hadn't resolved anything, and she knew that the situation wasn't going to be easily resolved. But despite her concerns, she wasn't ready to give him up just yet.

"Well, it would be a shame to waste the next few hours," she said, and let him lead her into the house.

Ashley was on her way to Megan's for a scheduled Friday night get-together with her sister and her cousin when Paige called to let her know that she was stuck at the office and wouldn't be able to make it. Ashley didn't question what had kept her late because she understood that Paige's commitment to her clients was one of the qualities that made her such an effective advocate for them, but she couldn't deny that she was disappointed.

She'd been hoping to talk to both Megan and Paige, to get an objective assessment of the situation with Cam, because after only three weeks, she was afraid that she'd already lost all objectivity where he was concerned. Still, she was optimistic that Megan might be able to shed some light on things, if she could find a delicate way to broach the subject.

But when Megan asked her what was new, she responded by blurting out, "I'm sleeping with Cam."

Her sister's eyes popped wide, then her lips curved. "Oh,

Paige is going to be *so* annoyed that she didn't come tonight." She helped herself to another slice of pizza. "Since when?"

Ashley frowned at her sister's question. "Why does the when matter?"

"Because Paige and I made a bet about when it would happen."

"You *expected* this to happen?"

Megan smiled. "Honey, you're probably the only one who didn't. After seeing you and Cam together, it wasn't a question of if, but when."

Ashley huffed out a breath. "Three weeks ago," she admitted.

"Damn. That means Paige wins." She looked at her sister with obvious disapproval. "*I* thought you would hold out longer than that."

Ashley squirmed. "Well, it's been a long time."

"And Cam has always known how to ring your bell." Megan took a long sip of her Sprite, then looked across the table. "So—how is it?"

"Spectacular," Ashley admitted.

Her sister grinned. "Good old Cam."

"But I didn't want to be having great sex with him," Ashley told her sister.

"You wanted to be having lousy sex with him?"

She sighed. "I wanted to be having purposeful sex with him."

"Purposeful?" Megan queried skeptically.

"For the purpose of procreation," she explained.

"You want to have Cam's baby?" There was more than a hint of concern in Megan's question.

"No," she denied. "I want to have *a* baby, and Cam has agreed to help me."

Her sister frowned.

"You obviously don't approve," Ashley noted.

"I don't understand," Megan admitted.

"I thought it was pretty self-explanatory."

"And if you get pregnant?"

Now it was Ashley's turn to frown. "Why are you even asking that question? You know I'd be ecstatic."

"But what would it mean for your relationship with Cam?" her sister wondered.

"Well, that's what I'm worried about, because this was never supposed to be a relationship."

"Just sex?" There was skepticism again—a lot of it.

"Yes," Ashley insisted.

"And you expected that Cam would politely bow out of your life after his stud service had been completed?"

Her frown deepened. "You don't have to make it sound so crude."

"Using pretty words won't change the intent," Megan warned. "*If* that truly is your intent."

"I was clear about what I wanted and Cam accepted the terms."

"Do you really believe that?" her sister challenged.

"Why wouldn't I?" Ashley asked warily.

"Because you've seen that man with his daughter, you know how completely devoted he is to her, and yet you've somehow managed to delude yourself into believing that he would turn his back on another child.

"Or maybe," Megan continued, "you let yourself believe it because you want the forever kind of tie that having a baby together would create."

Ashley was stunned by her sister's conclusion and immediately opened her mouth to deny it. But then she found herself wondering—could it be true? Had she only been deluding herself about what she wanted from Cam? Did she really want a future with him, a family with him?

"I have been such an idiot," she said, reaching for her drink.

"Love will do that," Megan said consolingly.

Love?

She nearly choked on her Diet Coke. Though she'd acknowledged that there was probably some truth in what her sister had said, she hadn't yet made the jump from accepting that she had feelings for Cam to putting a label on those feelings.

"Oh. My. God."

Megan looked at her, silently questioning.

"I *am* in love with him," she admitted.

"Again—probably not news to anyone but yourself," Megan told her.

"I thought I was being so smart. So careful."

"Honey, this is a *good* thing, not a catastrophe."

"That's a viewpoint exclusive to the happily married," Ashley told her. "The perspective of a woman who was in love with the same man once before is a little bit different."

"You were both young," her sister said gently.

"I know." Which didn't alter the fact that he'd trampled her heart and shattered her dreams. He'd known what she most wanted and taken it away from her.

And now he's trying to give it back to you.

She wasn't sure where that thought had come from, but she realized it was true. Whether or not Cam's decision to help her have a baby was a conscious effort to make amends, there was no denying that he was offering her everything she'd always wanted.

Not just a baby but, if Megan's theory was right, a family. A life and a future with Cam and Maddie and any other children they might have together.

"Maybe you're right," Ashley finally said to her sister. "Maybe this is a good thing."

"Now that we've established that," Megan said, as if her

conclusion was never in question, "is there anything else I should know?"

"I think I've made enough potentially life-altering revelations for one night," Ashley told her.

But the truth was, there was one more.

Her period was two days late.

Chapter Twelve

Ashley woke early Saturday morning feeling tired and crampy, but she still didn't have her period. She poured herself a glass of orange juice and swallowed her daily dose of Fedentropin and the prenatal vitamins she'd been taking since she and Cam started sleeping together.

According to all the books she'd read—and she'd read a lot of them—it was important to take the vitamins not just in the first trimester of pregnancy but even before conception to ensure the mother's body wasn't lacking in any essential nutrients required for her baby's healthy development. She laid a hand on her belly and thought about the tiny life that might already be growing inside of her. Cam's baby.

She knew it was too early to make any plans. She didn't even know for sure that she was pregnant. She was only a few days late and she hadn't even taken a home pregnancy test, so sharing her suspicions with Cam might seem a little premature.

But when she headed out for her usual morning walk, she found herself turning toward his house. Her heart was pounding as she made her way along the interlocking brick path that led to his front door. She still didn't know what she was going to say, or even if she would say anything, she was suddenly just anxious to see him.

She pressed the bell and heard the chime through the partially open living room window, then the sound of pounding footsteps. Maddie, she thought, with a smile.

The little girl opened the door just as Ashley heard an unfamiliar female voice call out from the background. "Madeline, you know you don't open the door unless you know who it is."

"It's Miss Ashley," Maddie called back, and pushed the door wider, giving Ashley a clear view down the hall.

A view that included a stunningly beautiful woman who didn't seem to be wearing anything more than a silky robe that fell to mid-thigh.

Ashley felt as if the bottom had dropped out of her stomach.

The woman's silky dark hair, delicate features and slim build clearly identified her as Maddie's mother. And Cam's ex-wife.

"Miss Ashley?" Danica questioned, moving toward the door without any apparent regard for or concern about her state of undress.

"She's my teacher," Maddie announced.

The other woman's perfectly shaped brows lifted. "Oh. Well, I'll have to apologize, Miss Ashley. We had a late night and you've caught us before we're all up and about for the day."

"No, I'm sorry," Ashley said. "I didn't mean to intrude."

"Daddy and I are going to make pancakes," Maddie announced, oblivious to the tension between the adults. "Do you want to stay and have breakfast with us?"

Ashley shook her head. "Thanks, but I, uh, already ate."

"You're more than welcome to join us," Danica said, as if she had every right to be inviting guests for breakfast in her ex-husband's home. "Cameron should be down from the shower in just a minute or two, and he really does make fabulous pancakes."

"I'm sure he does," Ashley said, because she'd never actually tasted *Cameron's* pancakes. Because he'd never made breakfast for her after spending the night in her bed. Because that wasn't the kind of relationship they had. "But I really can't stay."

Those brows lifted again, and Ashley knew the other woman was wondering why she'd stopped by in the first place. So she made a hasty retreat before her lover's ex-wife could ask the question she had no idea how to answer.

Cam had become accustomed to changing his plans at a moment's notice, because he believed that it was important for Madeline to spend time with her mother. So whenever Danica contacted him to say that she would be in town—whether she gave him a week's notice or called from the nearest airport—he tried to accommodate her. That didn't mean he didn't resent it.

But he'd never resented it more than when he got the call Friday night and had to rearrange his whole weekend schedule. A weekend that he'd planned to include a sleepover for Maddie at her grandparents' and a quiet, romantic evening at home for himself with Ashley. He definitely resented having to change those plans.

After breakfast Saturday morning, he suggested that Danica take Maddie to her ballet class. He figured it would give his ex-wife the opportunity to see how well her daughter's dancing was coming along and give Maddie some time alone with her mother. But Danica balked at the idea, claiming she would love to see Maddie dance but that she was uncomfortable driving in an unfamiliar city. So the three of them had gone to Maddie's dance class, then to Walton's for ice cream, then to the grocery store to pick up a few things. By the time they got back home, most of the day was gone.

Cam checked the answering machine, listened to the three messages that had recorded. The first was from his mother, just checking in, the second was a credit card company wanting to share important information about his account and the third was Maddie's friend Victoria.

Maddie overheard the last message and insisted on calling her friend back right away. Cam recited the number for her to dial, while Danica set up her laptop at the breakfast bar to check her e-mail.

Cam put the groceries away while Maddie chatted to her friend and Danica clicked away on her keyboard.

Maddie hung up the phone and skipped back into the kitchen. "Daddy, I need you to take me to Victoria's."

"First of all, you *ask* if I can take you to Victoria's," he told her. "Second, you have to get permission before you make plans. And third, you can't go to Victoria's today because your mom is here to visit with you."

Maddie glanced at her mother, who was engrossed in her electronic correspondence and oblivious to their conversation.

"She's working, and I want to play with Victoria."

His usually sweet-natured daughter wasn't prone to temper tantrums, but Cam sensed that this was one of the rare occasions when she was heading in that direction. "I know you're disappointed, Maddie," he said reasonably, "but it's not often that you have the opportunity to spend time with your mom so you need to take advantage of it while you can."

"She doesn't want to spend time with me," Maddie said.

"Even when I go to London, she sends me off to museums and zoos with Peggy. I want to play with Victoria."

The mention of London seemed to catch Danica's attention, because she glanced over at Maddie and frowned, but she didn't dispute her daughter's claim. And while Cam was disappointed to learn that Maddie had spent her time in London with her mother's assistant rather than Danica, he wasn't really surprised.

"How about a compromise?" he suggested to his daughter now.

"What's a compromise?"

"It's when two people who want different things both accept that they can't have what they want but agree on something in the middle."

Her brow furrowed as she tried to follow that explanation. "What's in the middle?"

"Well, in this case, it might be Victoria coming over here to play."

She considered that for a minute before she asked, "But what if she doesn't want to come here because she doesn't want to intrude?"

He wasn't sure what had precipitated that question, but he answered it anyway, "If you invite someone, it's not an intrusion."

"But I invited Miss Ashley to stay for pancakes and she said she didn't want to intrude."

Cam frowned. "When was this?"

"At breakfast."

"Today?"

She nodded.

He looked at Danica, directing his next question at her. "Ashley was here this morning?"

"Did I forget to mention that?" Danica said.

Cam narrowed his gaze on his ex-wife, but she only shrugged.

"I didn't realize she was here to see *you,*" she protested. "In fact, she didn't mention why she'd stopped by."

"Maddie, please call Victoria back and ask if she can come here to play."

Happy to accept his proposed compromise, she skipped off again.

"So who is Ashley?" Danica asked. "Because obviously she's someone more than Madeline's teacher."

"She's a friend."

"Our daughter seems quite taken with her," Danica noted.

"She's spent a lot of time with Ashley over the past few months."

"In the classroom—or here?"

He wasn't ashamed of his relationship with Ashley and he had no intention of hiding it from his ex-wife. On the other hand, he didn't feel as if he owed Danica any explanations, so he only asked, "Why the twenty questions?"

"I'm just curious about the woman you seem to have lined up to fill the role of stepmother in my daughter's life."

There was an unexpected edge to her voice, but Cam had learned a long time ago that Danica could manufacture whatever emotions were required to suit her purposes. "And I'm curious to know why you think spending maybe thirty days a year with your daughter gives you the right to turn everything upside-down when you do show up for a visit."

"If my being here is interfering with your life, I can go," she said coolly.

"You'd like me to say yes, wouldn't you? Then you could blame me for the lousy relationship you have with our daughter."

She looked away, but not before he saw her eyes fill with tears.

"Victoria's coming to play," Maddie announced, coming back to the kitchen. "Her mommy's going to drop her off so I'm going to sit on the porch to wait for her."

"Put your coat on, and make sure you stay on the porch." Cam reminded her.

"I will," she promised.

Danica watched her daughter walk away.

"No," she responded to his earlier question. "I know the lousy relationship I have with Madeline is entirely my fault."

He sighed. "You know it doesn't have to be like this. I would never deny you the opportunity to spend more time with Maddie."

"I know," she admitted. "But it's better this way. Really."

Cam didn't argue with her. He'd spent far too much time doing exactly that over the years and it had never changed anything. It made him wonder how he'd ever thought himself in love with Danica when it was apparent now that he'd never known her at all.

He pushed the thought, and the regrets, aside. He wasn't going to dwell on the mistakes of the past. He had too much to look forward to for the future—with Ashley.

Ashley was in the garage, up to her elbows in tangled Christmas lights, when Cam came up the walk. She'd been outside for a while, so her fingers were cold and struggling with the task. So far, she'd managed to untangle only half of one sixteen-foot strand.

Her frustration with the lights paled in comparison to her annoyance with him, though she wasn't entirely sure her annoyance was either rational or founded except that it was now after three o'clock in the afternoon and she'd been thinking about Cam being with his ex-wife for more than six hours.

He studied her for a moment, as if trying to figure out what she was doing, or maybe he didn't know what to say to her, either. But when he spoke, his voice was light, teasing.

"Jumping the gun, aren't you?"

Something she seemed to be doing a lot of these days. But all she said was, "I prefer not to be climbing a ladder when it's snowing."

"You shouldn't be climbing a ladder at all," he said. "I can do that for you."

"I appreciate the offer, but I don't need your help. I've been handling this particular task on my own for several years now and am more than capable of continuing to do so."

He tucked his hands in his pockets, rocked back on his heels. "You're annoyed with me."

She was, but she couldn't admit it because she had no right to be annoyed with him. So she shook her head. "No, I'm not."

"I heard you met my ex-wife this morning."

"Formal introductions weren't made, but yes, I met your ex-wife."

"What did she say to cause this mood?" he wanted to know.

"Nothing," she said, because it was true. "In fact, she was very pleasant."

He eyed her warily. "So why are you angry?"

She gave up trying to pretend that she wasn't. "Because she was in her robe and you were in the shower."

He took a moment to absorb her statement and the implications of it. When he responded, his tone was deliberate and even, as if he was trying to hold his own annoyance in check. "You don't honestly think I slept with Danica?"

She had thought that—if only for half a second. But that half a second had been long enough to make her question the relationship they'd only started to build, and make her wonder if she might lose him again.

"Ashley?" he prompted.

There was a definite edge in his voice, a dangerous glint in his eye, and she knew she'd been foolish to give in to her fears and insecurities for even that half-second.

"No," she finally responded. "At least, not when I think about it logically." Then she sighed and dumped the tangle of lights at her feet. "On the other hand, the door opens and there she is, and she's beautiful and half-naked and we never talked about exclusivity or lack of."

"I didn't think we needed to have a discussion," Cam said. "I thought the fact that we were sleeping together implied exclusivity."

"I don't assume anything," she said. "Not anymore."

His gaze narrowed. "Don't you dare compare me to that idiot you were engaged to."

"I'm not. At least, I'm trying not to. But I was the one who said this was just about sex, that I didn't want a relationship."

"Have you changed your mind?"

"No," she said, and immediately felt guilty for the lie. "Maybe. I don't know."

Cam picked up one end of a light strand and methodically began to unravel it. She wished she could do the same with the mess of emotions tangled inside of her. But every time she thought she'd figured out one thread, something happened to twist it up again.

"I just wish you'd told me that she was coming," she said, because coming face to face with the stunning woman he'd married had felt like a sucker punch.

"I would have told you if I'd known," he said gently.

She frowned at that. "You didn't?"

"Danica has a habit of calling at the last minute, showing up on a whim. And because Madeline gets little enough time with her mother, I let her."

She could hardly blame him for that, especially not after she'd encouraged him to facilitate more contact between mother and child.

"And then I showed up," she said, trying to look at the situation from his perspective. "How awkward was it for you to explain why Maddie's teacher was knocking at your door at nine o'clock on a Saturday morning?"

"Danica and I have been divorced for almost five years. She knows I've dated other women, just as I know she's dated other men. I don't have to explain anything to her."

Even so, Ashley knew the other woman had been curious about her visit. But she accepted his explanation for what it was, and tried to tamp down her own curiosity.

"Why did you come by this morning?" he asked her.

She couldn't—wouldn't—tell him the real reason. Not now. Not while Danica was in town and before anything had been confirmed.

"I was just thinking about you and Maddie," she said, because that was at least partially true.

He set aside one untangled and now neatly coiled string of lights. "And missing me?"

"No."

"I miss you," he said softly. "Whenever I wake up in the morning without you. Whenever I go to sleep at night without you. Whenever I think about you and you're not there, which happens about a hundred times a day, I miss you."

They were just words, but something about those words— or maybe it was the sincerity of his tone and the warmth in his eyes—made her heart soften, yearn. But all she said was, "Oh."

He smiled. "That surprises you, doesn't it?"

"A little."

"And scares you?" he guessed.

"More than a little," she admitted, but she knew that his feelings didn't scare her half as much as her own.

"Well, I just thought you should know," he told her.

She took the second string of lights from him. "It scares me," she said, "because I miss you, too. Sometimes."

Despite the obvious reluctance of her admission, he smiled, clearly pleased by her response. "That's a start." He touched his hand to her cheek, his palm warm against her skin. His smile faded. "You're freezing."

She shrugged. "I guess I've been out here for a while."

"Why don't we go in and put on a pot of coffee?"

She closed the garage door and followed him into the house.

Though she thought they'd cleared the air about his ex-wife's visit, mostly, there was still one specific concern gnawing at the back of her mind. She turned on the faucet and filled the pot with water and wondered if she dared ask Cam about it.

Paige had once told her that in relationships, as in a cross-examination at trial, you never ask a question you don't already know the answer to. Of equal importance was to never ask a question if the answer could hurt you. But she had to know.

When the coffee finished brewing, she poured two cups and slid one over the table to Cam before taking the seat across from him.

"Have you ever thought about getting back together with her?" she asked him.

"Danica?"

She nodded.

"No," he said.

The immediate and definitive response should have reassured her, but she wasn't able to relinquish her concerns so easily. "But she's Maddie's mother."

"Yes, she is," he agreed.

"And if she wanted to reconcile, wouldn't you want that for your daughter?"

"No," he said again.

"Why not?"

"Because we were never happy together, and that's not the kind of relationship example I want to set for my child."

She wanted to be satisfied by his explanation. It was logical and it answered her question, but for some reason she couldn't let it go. "You were in love with her once."

Cam set his cup down and met her gaze across the table.

She could tell he wasn't any happier than she was about the direction of their conversation, but like a train veering dangerously off-track, she couldn't seem to stop it.

"I wouldn't have married her if I wasn't," he admitted. "But, as it turned out, I didn't really know her and she didn't really know me, and when we finally got around to sharing all the intimate details that you should know about the person you marry, it was too late."

But whether he knew her or not, he'd fallen in love with her, and Danica was beautiful, sophisticated, ambitious—everything Ashley wasn't. "She obviously still cares about you."

"We have a child together," he reminded her. "That creates a bond that can't ever be broken."

Which was almost the same thing that Megan had said to her, but which took on a whole new meaning when applied to Cam and his ex-wife. And it made Ashley wonder if it might not be a mistake to tie herself to a man who was already tied to someone else.

Cam didn't know what else he could say to Ashley to alleviate the doubts he could see swirling in the depths of her violet eyes, and he mentally cursed his ex-wife again, adding bad timing to his usual complaints of selfishness and lack of consideration. Because just when he and Ashley had finally started to make progress in their relationship, Danica's unexpected appearance had put a damper on everything.

"But Maddie is the only reason we're still in contact," he continued his explanation. "There's nothing else between us anymore."

"I'm sorry if it seems like I was interrogating you," she said. "I was just caught off guard when Maddie opened the door and she was there."

"Does it bother you that she's staying at my house?"

"No," she said.

But he knew it was a lie. Because he knew that if Ashley's ex had suddenly taken up residence in her house, however temporarily, it sure as hell would bother him.

"It's only for a few days," he told her. "But I can check her into a hotel—"

"No," she said again. "If this is your usual arrangement, if it gives Maddie more time with her mother, then there's no reason to change it. But I have to admit, it bothers me that she'd rather be sleeping in your bed than down the hall."

"Whatever gave you that idea?" he asked cautiously.

"Are you going to deny that it's true?"

He wished he could. But he wouldn't lie to her and he wouldn't tiptoe around the truth. "She did imply that she didn't want to sleep in the spare room," he admitted. "But I clarified the situation for her."

"And why did it need clarification?"

He didn't know how to answer that question without landing himself in hotter water, so he said nothing.

"Because she's used to dropping in to your life when it's convenient for her—and back into your bed because that's convenient, too."

"It hasn't exactly been a pattern," he denied.

"But it's happened."

"I don't expect you to understand—"

"I do understand," she interrupted. "My friend Marilyn frequently has sex with her ex-husband because, to use her words, the itch needs to be scratched and it's safer to use a stick that's familiar for the task."

He winced at the harshness of the analogy, though he couldn't deny there was some truth in it.

"I haven't had sex with Danica in more than two years," he told her. "In fact, I haven't been with anyone at all in that time, until you. Do you want to know why?"

She shrugged.

"Because I got tired of sex that didn't mean anything. Because I wanted something more for myself." He slipped his arms around her waist, drew her closer. "Because I wanted to be with someone I care about."

"You're making this into something more complicated than it was supposed to be."

"So sue me."

"Paige is a lawyer," she reminded him. "Don't tempt me."

"Okay, I'll let you tempt me instead."

She tipped her head back so that her lips were only a whisper away from his. "Do you think I could?"

"You already have," he said, and carried her up to the bedroom.

Chapter Thirteen

Cam had told Ashley that Danica would only be in town for a few days, but at the end of the week, she was still there, still in Cam's house—sleeping down the hall from her ex-husband. And then one week turned into two, because—as she explained to Ashley when she came to school to pick up Maddie—she'd managed to settle a big case before trial, allowing her to extend her leave and spend more time with her family.

She hadn't said her *daughter,* but her *family.*

And the longer Danica stayed, the more Ashley worried that Cam might change his mind about wanting to reconcile with his ex-wife.

She knew she was being irrational, but from her perspective, Cam had chosen the other woman over her once already—when he'd left Ashley in Pinehurst and fallen in love with Danica.

Still, she had to give him an A for effort, because he continued to call her every night and to stop by whenever he had a chance. Of course, Danica kept him busy so that those chances were infrequent, but she didn't blame Cam for that. She knew he was only trying to facilitate the relationship between his daughter and her mother, but she couldn't deny that she missed spending time with him, and she missed making love with him.

She could call it having sex, but her conversation with her sister only a couple of weeks earlier had forced her to acknowledge the truth of her feelings for Cam. She was in love with him—and she was very much afraid that, for the second time in her life, she was going to lose him.

A fear that grew stronger every day through the week, until Friday night, when he showed up at her door.

"I thought Victoria was spending the night at your house with Maddie," Ashley said.

"She is," Cam agreed. "But it occurred to me that Danica should be able to handle two six-year-old girls for a few hours."

"Should?"

He shrugged. "They've got popcorn and movies—everything is good."

"So what are we going to do for a few hours?"

"We could make popcorn and watch a movie," he suggested. Which wasn't at all what she'd expected him to say. "Really?"

"Why do you sound so surprised?"

"I just figured you didn't come over here to watch a movie."

"I came over here to be with you, because I missed you."

And he sounded so sincere that her heart gave a little fluttery sigh, warning that she was in big trouble.

"I love making love with you," he told her, "but I love just being with you, too."

He'd used the word *love* three times in one sentence, but he hadn't actually said that he loved her. Of course, she hadn't said the words to him, either. Though she no longer had any doubts about the feelings in her heart, before she put it all on the line, she needed some more time to trust and believe that they could make their relationship work.

"In that case, I think I would enjoy watching a movie with you." She smiled. "Later."

When Cam sneaked out to see Ashley, he hadn't done so with the intention of getting her naked, but he sure as hell wasn't going to protest when things started moving in that direction. Even after several weeks, the attraction between them had not begun to wane and the intensity of their lovemaking had not diminished. And while he knew Ashley was hoping to get pregnant, he didn't believe her desire for a baby was the sole driving force behind her passion. No, the chemistry had been there twelve years ago and it was still there, and more powerful than ever.

But just as they were about to fall back onto Ashley's bed, his cell phone rang.

Cam swore under his breath as he released his hold on Ashley to reach into his pocket. CALL FROM HOME was on the display, and he glanced apologetically at her. "I'm sorry. I have to—"

"Don't apologize," she interrupted. "Of course you need to make sure everything's okay with your daughter."

He connected the call. "Maddie?"

"No, it's me."

Danica.

He frowned. "What's wrong?"

"Nothing. I just wanted to let you know that we're out of milk, so that you can pick some up on your way home."

He was silent, trying to decipher the hidden meaning behind the seemingly innocuous words.

"Cam?" she prompted, when he failed to respond.

"Yeah, I'm here. I just can't believe you called to ask me to pick up milk."

"Is that a problem?"

"No," he said, still not sure he wasn't missing something. "I'm just not sure when I'm going to be back."

"Oh." There was a not-so-subtle note of disapproval in her voice. "Madeline and Victoria wanted to make chocolate chip cookies, and we don't have any milk."

"You're baking cookies with the girls?"

"Is it so hard to believe?" she asked, the indignation in her tone confirming that he hadn't managed to hide the disbelief in his own.

"Actually, yes," he told her.

"Forget it, then," she said, obviously annoyed by his un-censored response. "I'll tell them that baking cookies will have to wait for another day."

"Have you even looked at the recipe?" he challenged.

"Of course I have."

"Because the recipe doesn't call for milk."

She didn't respond immediately, proving that she hadn't looked at the recipe, and that her request for milk wasn't the real reason for her call.

"Well, we want to drink milk with the cookies," she said.

"I'll pick some up before I come home," he told her. "But it won't be until later."

"Thank you," she said, and disconnected.

When Cameron turned around, Ashley had rebuttoned her shirt and was tugging a brush through her hair.

Obviously her mood had changed and the moment had passed.

"I'm sorry," he said again.

She just shook her head. "You don't even see what she's doing, do you?"

"Apparently not," he admitted cautiously.

She turned to face him. "She's playing the wife card."

"She's not my wife anymore," he reminded her.

"She called and asked you to pick up milk," Ashley said. "Which is the type of thing that a wife asks her husband to do."

"Even when we were married, she never made those kinds of calls. In fact, she probably wouldn't even have noticed if we were out of milk."

"And yet she called you now, knowing you were here, to ask."

"She doesn't know I'm here."

"You don't think so?" she challenged.

He frowned at the certainty in her tone. "How could she?"

"Your car is still in your driveway, which means that you didn't go too far, and, coincidentally, I live down the street."

"Danica doesn't play those kind of games," he said, but in the back of his mind, he wondered if he could be wrong.

"Neither do I," Ashley said.

It was the quiet resignation in her eyes that worried him more than the words or the tone.

"What are you saying?"

"I can't do this anymore, Cam. I won't be the other woman."

He was stunned. "Are you seriously asking me to choose between you and my ex-wife? Because if that's the case, let me remind you that she is my *ex*-wife."

Ashley took a step back. "I'm not asking you to choose at all. *I'm* making the choice this time, based on what's best for me, and that is to move on with my life without you in it."

"You don't mean that," he said, needing it to be true. Because to lose her again would be unbearable.

"I do mean it," she said softly. "Because you broke my heart once before, Cam, and I'm not going to give you a chance to do it again."

"What about the baby we were going to have?"

So much for Ashley's resolution not to let him break her heart again, because with only those words, it cracked wide open.

She looked away so he wouldn't see the distress she knew would be reflected in her eyes. Because having a baby with Cam had been her dream for so long, it broke her heart to admit that it just wasn't going to happen, that they were never going to be the family she wanted.

"Obviously it's a good thing I figured this out before I got pregnant."

"How do you know you're not pregnant?" he demanded.

"I got my period last week." She uttered the lie without compunction because she didn't want to put him in the position of having to choose—or maybe she didn't want to put herself in the position of being rejected again.

"Oh," he said, and she thought he sounded genuinely disappointed.

"It's for the best," she said, though it was another lie. Because she knew that if Cam even suspected the truth, he would never walk out the door. And she needed him to go. She needed to cut him out of her life so that she could get on with hers.

His gaze narrowed. "You expect me to believe that you've changed your mind about wanting a baby?"

She shook her head. "Of course not. I've just decided to revert to my original plan."

Because she'd jumped into this arrangement with Cam without thinking it through, without realizing that he already had responsibilities and obligations as a result of his first marriage. And she didn't want to spend the rest of her life in second place.

"You really want to have a baby fathered by a stranger?"

There was as much anger as disbelief in his tone, and it annoyed Ashley that he thought he had a right to be angry about anything. After all, she wasn't the one playing house with an ex-spouse.

"I'm not exactly planning on picking up someone in a bar," she reminded him.

"That would almost be preferable to having your baby's conception instigated by a catheter," he shot back.

"Then I'll be sure to keep that as a backup plan," she said coolly.

"Don't do this, Ashley." He sounded more worried than angry now, as if he'd finally realized that she meant what she'd said. "Don't shut me out of your life."

And she did mean what she'd said, even if the thought of watching him walk out on her once more made her heart break all over again. But she had to be strong—or at least make him believe that she was. It was the only way she would get through this.

"I was never looking for a relationship," she reminded him. "You were the one who tried to turn this into something more."

"Because I care about you." He took her hands, as if the physical connection would help her to believe the words he spoke. "I've always cared about you."

And she did believe that he cared about her. But she *loved* him, and she wouldn't settle for any less than being loved in return. Not this time.

"If you really care about me, you'll accept that this is my choice."

Cam had no intention of accepting Ashley's decision. At least not without doing everything he could to change her mind. But first he came to some conclusions of his own.

Before Danica left Pinehurst for Chicago, where she would be working on a corporate merger, he decided to set some guidelines and establish firm boundaries to govern future interactions with his ex-wife. For starters, he wanted Danica to commit to seeing Maddie at least four times a year on a regular schedule. He assured her that he would never deny requests for additional visitation, but he'd come to realize that one of the reasons Maddie was so despondent whenever she had to say goodbye to her mother was that she never knew when she would see her again. He also informed Danica that she would have to arrange for her own accommodations for future visits, with Maddie staying overnight with her mother if that was what they both wanted.

To his surprise, Danica didn't object to any of his terms. And when all was said and done, he felt good about the decisions they'd made. He only wished they'd made those same decisions six months earlier, or at least before Ashley had concluded that she didn't want to be with a man who was still struggling to fix the mistakes of his past.

As he sat with Maddie in the rooftop parking lot of the airport to watch his ex-wife's plane lift into the air, he was thinking of Ashley. Missing Ashley.

Apparently Maddie was, too, because he'd barely pulled out of the parking lot when she asked, "Can we go see Ashley now?"

"Oh, honey." He glanced at the clock on the dash. "It's too late to go visiting anyone tonight."

"But you're still friends with her, aren't you? You still like her, don't you?"

"Of course," he said.

But the truth was, he had no idea if he and Ashley were still friends, and he wanted to be so much more. And although he did like her, that word didn't begin to describe the depth of his feelings for her.

"Can we see her tomorrow?" Maddie pressed.

"You will see her tomorrow—at school," he reminded her.

"I like when she comes to visit us at home because then I get to call her Ashley instead of Miss Ashley."

The dropping of the title was something Ashley and

Maddie had decided, and though he worried that his daughter might slip up at school one day, so far she'd been careful. Probably because she was so thrilled to be on a first-name basis with her teacher outside of school that she wouldn't do anything to jeopardize the privilege.

Of course, she didn't know that her father had screwed everything up for her—and he was still hoping that he might find a way to fix it before she ever found out.

"But I am excited about going to school tomorrow," Maddie continued, oblivious to his inner turmoil. "Because we're going to make up our own fairy tales."

"That sounds like an ambitious project."

"Ashley—*Miss* Ashley—says the best stories are those that show imagination and heart. I thought she was talking about the pictures, and I asked her how to draw a picture of imagination, but she explained that imagination is making something up—telling about something that isn't real but that you can see in your mind.

"Can you see things in your mind, Daddy?"

"I guess I can sometimes."

"Then you know how to use your imagination," she told him.

Cam only wished he could imagine the right scenario to get Ashley back in his life.

Instead of their usual brunch, Ashley was meeting her sister and her cousin for a late lunch because Paige was babysitting while a friend went to an appointment. Since she had some time before she was due to meet them, Ashley decided to wander through some of the shops on Rockton Street.

She paused outside of Hush, Little Baby, her attention caught by the gorgeous cherrywood crib and dressing table on display. A recent visit to Dr. Alex had confirmed that the baby she'd wanted for so long would be a reality by the end of next summer, and though she knew it was too early in her pregnancy to think about making any major purchases, she couldn't resist browsing. Pushing open the door, she stepped inside and found that the store was a lot bigger than it appeared from the front and that the enormous space was divided into several distinctly themed rooms.

She walked past a hugely pregnant woman and her obviously adoring husband discussing infant car seats with one of the salesladies and tried not to think about the fact that, when it came time for her to pick out a car seat, she would be making the decision on her own. She would be making all of the decisions; she would bear all of the responsibilities. And that was okay, because it was her choice. But she knew that her child would miss out on so much if Cam wasn't part of his or her life.

Pushing the thought aside, she moved into the first room. This one had a sports focus, with dark furniture, bold plaid fabrics and an assortment of books and outfits for sale that continued the theme. She picked up a miniature baseball uniform displayed beside a board book version of "Casey at the Bat."

Beyond the sports room was a prehistoric setting, with everything and anything dinosaur. Then a vibrant circus-themed room, which she chose to bypass. Although she was sure the bright, primary colors would appeal to a child, there was something about perpetually grinning clown faces that had always creeped her out.

And then she discovered the fairy tale room, where everything was frilly and feminine—a little girl's dream. Neatly tucked inside the open drawer of a glossy white wardrobe was a frilly little tutu and a pair of tiny pink ballet slippers. She picked up the shoes, marveling at the detail and delicacy, and found herself thinking about Maddie, who loved to twirl and pirouette in her sock feet on the kitchen floor. And Ashley wondered if maybe her daughter would display the same enthusiasm some day, inspired by a tiny pair of ballet slippers just like the ones she was holding.

But it was too early in her pregnancy to begin speculating about whether the baby she was carrying was a boy or a girl, so it was more than a little premature to be thinking about Little League and dreaming of ballet recitals. With a soft, regretful sigh, she put the shoes down and, turning, nearly collided with Cam's mother.

"This is my favorite room in the whole store," Gayle told her, her voice low as if she was confessing something she shouldn't.

"It's my first time in here," Ashley admitted. "But I'm amazed."

"Then I know you'll be back," Gayle said. "Because every time there's something new and different but always wonderful."

"I'll definitely be back," Ashley said, then felt her cheeks color, a reaction that was more telling than her words. But she recovered quickly with the explantion, "Because my sister's pregnant."

"Ashley!" Maddie's voice rang out from across the room, and the little girl skipped over, carrying a floppy-eared bunny that had obviously caught her eye.

Ashley turned, grateful for the interruption that allowed her to pull her foot out of her mouth.

"We're shopping for baby stuff," Maddie told her. "'Cause my aunt Sherry's going to get a baby."

"Well, that's exciting news," Ashley said.

"Are you going to get a baby, too?"

Ashley sucked in a breath, caught off guard by the child's innocent question. And she knew that's all it was—the simple curiosity of a six-year-old. "Oh. Someday, I hope." She forced a smile. "But before I have a baby, I'm going to have a niece or a nephew."

"I'm getting a cousin," Maddie said proudly.

"A cousin who will be living in Florida," Gayle noted with obvious disappointment. "I don't know why it is that my kids had to go so far away to have their kids. I hate being a long-distance grandparent."

"Well, at least Cam and Maddie are home now," Ashley said, as the child wandered off again.

Gayle smiled as she kept a watchful eye on her grand-daughter. "And I'm so grateful for that."

"Look at these, Grandma." Maddie was back again, this time with the little ballet slippers Ashley had recently admired. "Can we get these so the baby can be a dancer like me?"

Gayle looked at the price tag, winced. "Honey, she won't even be walking, never mind dancing when she's wearing shoes that size."

"But they're so pretty." Maddie stroked a finger over the satiny toe.

"And I am such a sucker," her grandmother laughed as she put the shoes into the basket she carried over one arm. "I can't tell you how much time—and money—I spent in here when Maddie was a baby. I don't think a week went by that I wasn't sending a sleeper or a dress or something out to her. Of course, Cam now blames me for his daughter being a clothes horse, but I figure it's a grandma's job to spoil the little ones."

"I take it Sherry's expecting a girl?" Ashley prompted.

"Oh, yes. She told me last night. I'd have started shopping as soon as I got the news, except that the store was already closed for the day," Gayle admitted.

"I'm glad it's a girl. Girls are better than boys," Maddie declared. "I think a sister would be better than a cousin, but I have to settle for a cousin because daddies can't have babies and my mommy isn't really the nurchring type."

"Maddie," her grandmother admonished gently.

"That's what you told Grandpa."

"I'm sure I did," Gayle admitted in an undertone to Ashley. "But I wouldn't have said it if I'd known she was within hearing distance."

Ashley smiled. "I teach first grade," she reminded the older woman. "Believe me, I understand only too well how they can forget direct instruction but recite verbatim something they should never have overheard."

"What's nurchring?" Maddie asked Ashley.

"I think you mean *nurturing*," she said, scrambling to come up with a definition that wouldn't paint the little girl's mother in a completely negative light. "And it means to, uh, help grow or develop."

"Daddy says I grow like a weed, so maybe I don't need any more nurchring," Maddie decided. "Babies need help because they start out small, but I bet I could help."

"I'm sure you'd be a very big help," Ashley said, somehow forcing the words out through the tightness in her throat. And because she knew she would have a complete meltdown if she didn't get out of the store in the next thirty seconds, she said, "I have to run. I'm meeting Megan and Paige for lunch."

Then she fled, leaving Cam's daughter staring after her, and holding a huge piece of her heart.

Cam frowned at the stack of folders on his desk. It was almost seven o'clock, the last patient had walked out the door more than an hour earlier and he still had another hour or more of paperwork to finish. Thankfully his mother had agreed to take Maddie to ballet class so that he could stay late and try to catch up, but he refused to stay past eight o'clock—his daughter's bedtime.

He had been a part of her bedtime routine from the day she was born. Of course, the routine then had been much simpler:

a bottle and a cuddle—no snacks, drinks, checks for under-the-bed-monsters or stories required. But no matter how much the routine had changed and expanded over the years, Cam continued to cherish those quiet moments with his daughter.

On a few occasions, when Ashley had been over as Maddie was getting ready for bed, his daughter had asked her teacher to do story time instead. Cam wasn't really offended by her claims that Ashley told "the best stories" because he'd only had to listen to her once to know it was true.

He missed those story times. Or maybe he just missed Ashley.

Okay, no maybe about it—he *did* miss Ashley. And he was thinking, hoping, that if he gave her some time, she would soon realize that she missed him, too.

He opened the next folder on top of the pile, determined to push all thoughts of Ashley out of his mind and focus on his work so that he could be home for Maddie's bedtime.

Andy Robichaud was the name on the file. The elderly gentleman had come in a few weeks earlier, complaining of frequent and painful urination. Cam knew the cause could be something as simple as a urinary tract infection or as complicated as prostate cancer, so he'd ordered a series of tests to correctly identify the root of the problem.

The report from PDA Labs was on the top. He picked it up and skimmed the codes, the numbers, and struggled to make sense of the results. Because according to the paper, Mr. Robichaud was pregnant.

The report he was reading obviously belonged in someone else's file, not in that of a seventy-nine-year-old man—unless his patient was truly a medical miracle.

He was smiling at that impossibility when his gaze automatically shifted to the patient ID box at the top of the page. His smile slipped.

The test results were Ashley's.

Chapter Fourteen

When Ashley got home from her book club meeting Friday night, Cam was sitting in the dark on her front porch. If she'd been able to see him, she might have wondered why he was there. But she'd forgotten to leave the exterior lights on again and it was only when she stepped onto the path leading to the door that the sensor lights revealed his presence.

"Why didn't you tell me?" he demanded.

Her heart had jolted at the sight of him and now pounded crazily inside of her chest. It wasn't simply because she hadn't seem him in a while, but that she'd never seen him like this— his eyes hard, his jaw set, anger practically radiating off of him in waves.

And she immediately knew, without having to ask, what he was referring to. She swallowed. "How did you find out?"

"I hardly think that's the issue here."

Though her hands were shaking, she managed to slide her

key into the lock. "I assume you want to come in and talk about this."

"I'd say that a conversation is long overdue."

She dropped her coat and her purse inside the door, conscious of Cam following close on her heels as she made her way into the living room, turning on lights as she went and desperately trying to find the words to explain her deception.

"Did Eli tell you?" she finally asked.

"You know he would never breach doctor-patient confidentiality."

"Then how—"

"Your test results were misfiled. I might not have realized the error except that I've never known a seventy-nine-year-old man's blood work to reveal HCG."

"Oh."

"Now tell me why you didn't tell me," he challenged.

"I was going to," she hedged.

"When?"

"Even before I knew for certain that I was pregnant, I was so excited about the possibility that I wanted to share it with you."

"When was that?" he demanded to know.

She swallowed. "The day that I first met your ex-wife."

"That was almost three weeks ago."

"I know. But the longer she stayed, the more time she spent with you and Maddie, the more I started to doubt our relationship. Which I know doesn't make any sense," she admitted, "because I'm the one who said I didn't want a relationship and that Maddie should spend more time with her mother. But just when I started thinking that maybe we could be a family— you and Maddie and me and the baby—Danica showed up and reminded me that you already had a family."

"My marriage was never a secret," he pointed out.

"I know, but it was in the past and your ex-wife was on another continent. And then suddenly she was here and I decided I would rather raise my baby alone than let him know that he was your second choice."

"Why would you ever think something like that?" he demanded.

"Because I know what it feels like to be the runner-up. The bridesmaid instead of the bride."

"What are you talking about?"

"I fell in love with you when I was fifteen," she reminded him. "And during the two years that we were together, you told me you loved me, too. But when you graduated, you claimed that you weren't ready for a serious relationship, that you needed to concentrate on your studies. So I waited. You went away to college, then to med school, and I waited. Because I loved you. Then I found out that while I was waiting, you had married someone else."

"Because I was young and stupid and I foolishly thought that marrying someone else—someone who was completely unlike you—would finally help me forget about you.

"But it didn't work. I never forgot about you, Ashley. And I never stopped loving you. And when I agreed to go along with your plan to have a baby, it was only because I hoped that, by the time you got pregnant, you'd realize we should be together.

"Except that isn't quite how it happened, is it? As soon as you realized you were pregnant, you cut me out of your life. You never wanted me, you just wanted a baby."

His tone was so cold, so icily unforgiving, that she shivered. And because she knew that she was solely responsible for his anger, she didn't dispute his accusation. She didn't tell him that the truth was, she'd wanted everything.

Even if she hadn't realized it at the time, she'd wanted him and Maddie and their baby. But to admit that now would give him the power to destroy her pride along with her heart. And her pride was all she had left now.

"Because you were never going to let me be part of your family," she shot back.

"That's ridiculous."

"Every time I tried to include Maddie in our plans, you made other arrangements for her. Apparently I'm good enough to sleep with you, but you don't want me getting too close to your daughter."

"Maybe I just needed to know that you wanted to be with me for me, and not because of Maddie."

"You know me better than that."

"Apparently I don't, because I would never have expected you to keep the news of your pregnancy from me."

"Okay, I should have told you," she admitted. "Is that what you wanted me to say? Is that why you're here?"

"It's a start," he agreed.

"So where do we go from here? What are we going to do now?"

He didn't miss a beat. "Now we're going to get married."

She stared at him, stunned. "You want to get married?"

"Under the circumstances, it seems like a reasonable solution."

"Under the circumstances, it's completely ridiculous."

His jaw set. "Courts have pretty clear views on parental rights," he warned. "And I'm not going to let you cut me out of my child's life."

She managed to hold back the tears but couldn't hold back the words that were filled with anguish and torn from her heart. "You already took away my hopes and my dreams once, I'm not going to let you take *my* baby."

"*Our* baby," he said, but there was no warmth in his tone, only accusation.

She swiped a tear from her cheek. "Why are you doing this?"

"You can ask me that when you were the one who tried to trick me into getting you pregnant?" he asked scornfully.

She swallowed, but the guilt and the regrets stuck in her throat, practically choking her. "But I couldn't follow through with it."

"Except that you *are* pregnant," he pointed out.

"And I got that way with your consent and cooperation," she reminded him.

"Then you lied to me, telling me you weren't pregnant when you were."

"I didn't know for sure that I was!"

She was yelling at him. She'd never screamed at anyone before, and she was appalled by her behavior, ashamed of the out-of-control emotions that were churning inside of her.

"Look at us, Cam." She spoke softly, carefully, now. "We can't even have a rational conversation about this and you think we should get married?"

He took a step closer and cupped her face in his palms, his thumbs brushing away the tears she didn't even realize had spilled onto her cheeks. And then his mouth was on hers, and he was kissing her softly, slowly, deeply.

Her eyes drifted shut, her lips parted, her body yielded.

This was crazy. Complete insanity. She knew that, and yet, she couldn't seem to stop kissing him back.

She'd felt his absence from her life keenly in the past few weeks. And it wasn't just the physical aspect of their relationship that she missed, although there was no doubt she missed that as her pregnancy hormones seemed to have kicked into high gear, making her ache for him. But she'd missed so much more than that, too. The brief conversations they used to share when he picked Maddie up from school; their late night phone calls. Walks at Eagle Point Park; lazy Saturday mornings; Sunday afternoon matinees. In just a few short months, he'd become an integral part of her life again, and letting him go—even if it had been her decision—had ripped a hole in her heart.

But now he was here, holding on to her as if he never meant to let her go. And she was holding on to him, too.

When he finally eased his lips away from hers, he said, "Yes, I think we should get married."

"Wow. This is even better than last week's *Desperate Housewives*."

Ashley and Cam both turned to find Paige leaning against the doorjamb.

"I let myself in," she explained, "because it was apparent that nobody was going to respond to the bell."

Ashley didn't know if she was embarrassed to have been part of the scene her cousin walked in on or simply grateful that Paige had walked in. Because without the interruption, Ashley couldn't be certain she wouldn't have ended up back in bed with Cam—which is what had started this whole mess in the first place.

"I didn't think you were coming this weekend," she said.

"Change of plans."

"Well, your timing sucks," Cam told her.

She lifted a brow. "I really didn't mean to interrupt, but I thought you should know I was here before things moved beyond a PG-13 rating."

"Always happy to entertain you," Ashley said dryly.

Her cousin smiled, but Ashley noted the genuine concern and silent questions in her eyes.

"I should go," Cam said to Ashley, the focused intensity of his gaze warning that they still had a lot of unfinished business. "My mom's watching Maddie and I'm already later getting home than I told her I would be."

She nodded and followed him to the door, but it was only after she'd locked up behind him that she realized how much her knees were shaking.

"What was *that* all about?" Paige asked when she returned to the living room.

"I don't even know where to begin," Ashley admitted.

"Okay, let's start with Cam wanting to marry you."

She sighed. "Only because I'm pregnant."

Though Paige raised her eyebrows at that revelation, all she said was, "Knowing how much you've always wanted a baby, and how much you've always loved Cam, I'm not seeing a downside here."

"All I wanted was a baby. I didn't factor a husband anywhere into the equation, and Cam led me to believe that it would be up to me to decide what role—if any—he would play in our baby's life. And now that I am pregnant, he's changed his tune. Now it's all about his rights as the father. I didn't want a father—I wanted a sperm donor."

Paige didn't say anything.

Ashley swiped at more tears that had spilled onto her cheeks. "I can't believe I've made such a mess of everything."

"You only think it's a mess because it's not playing out the way you expected, because you didn't see that your plan was inherently flawed from the beginning."

Paige went to the freezer and pulled out a pint of Walton's chocolate fudge brownie ice cream. She got two spoons out of the drawer, then put one back when she peeled off the lid and realized there wasn't very much ice cream left.

Ashley frowned; Paige shrugged.

"I know pregnant women crave ice cream," she explained. "But sexually deprived women need chocolate. The fact that you are pregnant proves that you are not sexually deprived, ergo the pitiful amount of ice cream left in this container is mine."

"You can have the ice cream," Ashley said. "So long as you explain why you didn't warn me that this could happen."

Her cousin dipped her spoon into the ice cream. "Because you would have used it as an excuse to end your relationship before it had even begun, before you accepted that you never stopped loving Cam."

"Right now, I *hate* Cam."

"Love—hate." She licked the spoon. "Fine line."

Ashley shook her head. "I really hate him."

"You should have seen things from where I was standing. One minute you're spitting mad at each other, the next you're locked together in a steamy embrace." She fanned her face with her hand. "It was like watching a *really* hot movie."

"You're warped."

Her cousin grinned. "Seriously, Ash, that kind of passion is…inspiring. And all too rare."

"I don't want that kind of passion," Ashley lied. "And I sure as heck don't want Cam Turcotte barging into my life and telling me what to do."

"I could put up with some barging if it came with that kind of kissing."

"Then why don't *you* marry Cam?"

"He didn't ask me."

"And he only asked me because I'm going to have his baby."

"Congratulations, by the way."

Ashley allowed herself a smile. "Thanks."

"So when is due-day?"

"July twenty-ninth."

"Your mother will be happy."

"Why?" Ashley asked cautiously.

"Because she'll have a lot more time to plan your wedding than she had for Megan's."

"There's not going to be a wedding."

"That's not the impression I got from Cam."

"Well, Cam's already had one wedding, so that should be enough for him."

"Is that what this is really about? Are you still determined to punish him for finding someone else?"

"Do you really think I'm that petty?"

"I don't think you're petty at all," her cousin assured her. "But I also don't think you've ever been able to think clearly where Cam Turcotte is concerned."

"Well, forgive me for wanting to get married for reasons other than the fact that I'm pregnant."

"How about the fact that you love him?"

"I loved him once before, too," she admitted. "And he broke my heart when he left me."

And what she'd felt for Cam then was barely a shadow of what she felt now. Getting to know the man he'd become had forced her to let go of her infatuation with the boy he'd been and, in the process, her feelings had begun to change. The attraction was sharper, the chemistry stronger, the affection deeper.

And it worried her, that if she could love him so much more, he would have the power to hurt her even more. So she refused to give him that power.

Because Cam had moved away from home when he was nineteen, he'd learned at an early age to make his own choices and to live with the consequences—both good and bad—of those choices. Since coming home, he'd begun to appreciate the wisdom and experience his parents had to offer, and he'd found himself turning to them when he had questions or concerns about parenting or sometimes just to get a second opinion about something.

And that was why he went to his father's workshop Saturday morning.

Rob Turcotte was a finish carpenter by trade and by choice, and he'd taught his son that a job didn't feel like work if you loved the career you chose. It was a philosophy that was reflected in everything he did.

Cam mentally tried to assemble the various pieces of wood scattered on the table into some recognizable shape, then finally gave up and asked, "What are you making?"

"A cradle."

For half a second, Cam wondered if his father already knew what he'd come to talk to him about. Then he remembered his sister was expecting her first child—an exciting announcement but one that had been relegated to the back of his mind because he had more pressing concerns.

"For Sherry's baby?"

His father nodded. "Just like I made one for Maddie."

"She uses it for her dolls," Cam said, then wondered if he should have admitted that he let his daughter play with such a painstakingly crafted heirloom.

But his father, ever practical, said, "No reason to tuck it away in an attic to gather dust."

Cam watched him work for several minutes, checking edges, sanding rough spots. "It seems like a lot of work for a piece of furniture that's used for such a short time."

"It's a labor of love. And who knows? Maybe you'll have use for Maddie's cradle again someday."

"Maybe sooner than you think," Cam told him. "Ashley's pregnant."

Rob carefully set a delicate spindle down on the workbench before he met his son's gaze. "Is this what you wanted?"

Cam sighed. "It's what we both wanted. But now we can't seem to agree on where to go from here."

His father picked up a small sanding block and carefully began smoothing the rough edge of the wood.

"I want to marry her," Cam told him.

Rob nodded. "Seems reasonable."

"Ashley doesn't think so," he grumbled.

"She doesn't strike me as an unreasonable woman."

"About this, she's being completely unreasonable."

He paced the workshop while his dad sanded, and told him everything about their agreement.

"So you agreed, from the beginning, that you would make no claims with respect to the baby?" Rob asked.

Cam frowned. "I had to. It was the only way Ashley would include me in her plans."

"And now you want to change those plans?"

"She's carrying my child."

"I got that," his dad said. "But the fact remains that you set the terms and now you're pushing her to change them."

"Because I love her!"

His father lifted his brows. "Have you said those words to Ashley? And hopefully not shouted them at her."

Cam dropped his head into his hands. "I've really messed this up, haven't I?"

"It certainly seems that way."

"You know, that wasn't quite what I had in mind when I came in here for some fatherly advice."

His dad's only response was to ask, "When did you realize you were in love with Ashley?"

"When I saw her at the reunion," Cam admitted, though it had taken a long time after before he'd admitted as much to himself.

"So when you found out that Ashley wanted to have a baby, why didn't you just say, hey, that's convenient, because I'm in love with you anyway so we should get married and have a family together?"

"Because she would have thought I was a lunatic."

"Because she wasn't ready to accept your feelings?"

He nodded.

"And you knew that if you pushed her for too much too soon…." his dad prompted.

"I would push her away." Cam sighed as the point his father was trying to make finally became clear. "And that's what I'm doing now."

"Figured a man who graduated summa cum laude from medical school had to have at least half a brain," his father said.

"So what am I supposed to do—just back off and let her have this baby on her own?"

"That is what you said you'd do," his father reminded him.

"But—" Cam snapped his jaw shut as part of a long-ago conversation with Ashley played back inside his head.

"Trevor didn't break my heart. He broke my trust."

"And that takes longer to heal."

Cam had broken both her heart *and* her trust. Maybe Ashley did love him, but she was hurt and angry and scared, and if they were ever going to have a future together, he would have to earn her forgiveness.

And he knew that wasn't going to be easy.

When Greg Stafford showed up at her door the Tuesday night before Thanksgiving, Ashley wasn't just surprised, she was wary. She would say that she and the school principal had a friendly relationship, but she wouldn't say that they were friends.

Her trepidation increased when he said, "I apologize for bothering you at home, but I wanted to keep this conversation unofficial."

"Of course," she agreed, opening the door to invite him in.

She offered him coffee, which he declined, obviously not wanting to prolong his visit—the reason for which was still a mystery to her.

"I don't know how to delicately broach the subject," Greg

finally admitted, "so I'm just going to ask you point-blank. Is Cameron Turcotte the father of your baby?"

Ashley really wished he'd accepted her offer of coffee, because then she would be busy doing something and not just staring at him with a guilty flush staining her cheeks. "Where did you hear that?"

"It doesn't matter where I heard it," her principal said. "I'm asking you if it's true."

She'd told her principal about her pregnancy so that he would understand why she was taking a leave of absence at the end of the current school year, but she hadn't given him any details. And she swallowed nervously before answering his question now. "Yes."

"Are you going to marry him?"

She opened her mouth and, as if he knew that she was going to respond in the negative, Greg narrowed his gaze on her. "You might want to give that question some thought before you answer."

"We talked about the fact that I wanted to have a baby," she reminded him. "And you didn't express any concern about the fact that I wasn't married."

"Because you led me to believe that you were going to pursue alternate methods of conception."

"Why does it matter how I got pregnant?"

"It only matters if you're having an affair with the father of one of your students, which you just admitted that you are."

"Not having, had," she amended, though she suspected that the relationship being in the past wouldn't make a difference to her boss. "And we were both single, consenting adults."

Greg's sigh confirmed the fact. "Your personal life is just that," he told her. "Until someone brings it to the attention of the school board or the trustees. If that happens, it might be difficult for me to justify your position at the Parkdale."

She swallowed. "Are you threatening to fire me?"

"No." He sounded as shocked as she felt. "You have to know how much I enjoy having you on my staff, and how much the kids love you. But if the details of your relationship with Dr. Turcotte were revealed, the matter could be taken out of my hands."

"How did you find out?" she asked him.

"I got an anonymous phone call from someone. A woman. I don't believe your personal life is any of my business," he assured her. "But I couldn't ignore what she told me."

As soon as Greg said he'd spoken to a woman, Ashley instinctively knew it was Danica who had called. What she couldn't guess was why. What did the other woman hope to gain by exposing Ashley's relationship with Cameron? Or was it simply a power play—another chance to show Ashley that she still knew how to exert control over her ex-husband's life?

Ashley had the opportunity to answer at least some of her questions when she went to Walton's to pick up a couple of pints of ice cream the next day. It was her pitiful contribution to Thanksgiving dinner at Megan and Gage's house—a gathering that would include, in addition to the hosts, Ashley, Paige, Gage's parents, his brother and sister-in-law and their four kids, and Ashley and Megan's mother and her new husband.

When Ashley had commented on the size of the guest list, her sister had assured her that there was room for Cameron and Maddie, too. But Ashley knew that wasn't an option— not right now. She was still furious with Cam, still reeling from the fact that she'd barely had a chance to process the news of her pregnancy and he was threatening to sue for custody of a child who wasn't even close to being born.

Yes, she'd been furious and hurt, but she shouldn't have been surprised. Because, as her sister had so astutely pointed out, a man as devoted to one child as Cam was to Maddie would never turn his back on another. Maybe he'd misled her, but she was guilty of seeing what she wanted to see—or maybe not seeing anything beyond her own desires—and her reaction to his threat had been purely emotional and completely unreasonable.

Over the past couple of weeks, she'd finally accepted that she and Cam would need to find a way to work together for the sake of their child. And maybe they would find a way back to one another in the process. But first she had to get through the holiday.

While she was at Walton's, she ran into Danica, who was also picking up ice cream to go. It was ironic that, only a couple of months earlier, Ashley had suggested to Cam that Maddie should see more of her mother. Now Ashley was wishing Cam's ex-wife would just go back to England and stay there forever.

But she put a smile on her face and asked, "Are you in town to spend the holiday with Maddie?"

Danica nodded. "Just until Friday, then I'm back to Chicago, working on a corporate merger."

"I would have thought something like that would keep you so busy you wouldn't have time to stir up trouble for others."

The other woman shrugged, not even bothering to deny the accusation. "It seemed obvious to me that something had to be done to propel you and Cam forward."

"How does jeopardizing my job help either of us?"

Danica waved a hand dismissively. "They can't actually fire you."

"They could transfer me to another school."

"If you married Cameron, they'd have no reason to transfer you."

Ashley was as stunned by the suggestion as she was

annoyed by the other woman's machinations, and more than a little wary. The last time she'd been in town, Danica had focused her efforts on interfering in her ex-husband's new relationship. Was it really possible that she was now trying to push Ashley and Cam back together? And if so, why?

"You're assuming he's asked."

The other woman laughed. "I was married to the man once, remember?"

As if that was something Ashley was likely to forget.

"I know only too well how honorable and how committed to family he is," Danica reminded her. "And if I had to guess, I would say that 'marry me' were the first words out of his mouth when he learned you were pregnant. What I can't fathom is why you turned him down."

Ashley still wasn't sure that she should trust Cam's ex-wife, but the other woman's questions made her think, and made her wonder if she'd been too hasty in closing the door on a future with Cam. And though she'd had no intention of sharing her fears and concerns, she heard herself ask, "Would you want to marry a man who only proposed because you were pregnant?"

"I lied about being pregnant to get Cam to marry me," his ex-wife informed her.

Her shock must have been evident, because one corner of Danica's mouth lifted in a half smile. "He didn't tell you that, did he?"

Ashley shook her head.

"I was in love with him. Foolishly, perhaps, because it's obvious now that we were totally ill-suited for one another. But at the time, totally and completely. And when he started talking about coming back here and doing his internship in Pinehurst, I panicked. It was as if I knew, even without ever hearing him speak your name, that if he came home, I would lose him."

"So you told him you were pregnant?" Ashley was stunned by the audacity, then realized her own actions of late were hardly above reproach.

"And he, predictably, stepped right up to the plate," Danica told her.

She didn't know how to respond to this revelation; she didn't dare let herself think about how differently her life and Cameron's might both have turned out if Danica had never uttered those words. "What happened when he found out the truth?"

"He didn't—not for a long time. I told him I'd miscarried—" she looked away, and Ashley knew that Danica wasn't as blasé about her own behavior as she wanted to appear "—and he accepted that explanation."

"And then you did get pregnant."

Danica nodded. "And totally freaked. But he probably didn't tell you that, either."

She shook her head. "He said that the pregnancy was… unexpected."

"Unexpected," she agreed. "And unwelcome. I didn't want a baby. Not at that point in my life or our marriage, not ever."

"Why?"

"Long, boring story." Danica waved a hand dismissively. "My mother was unreasonable, demanding and abusive. My grandmother was the same, but also a drunk."

Ashley didn't have any trouble reading between the lines, and she felt an instinctive surge of sympathy for the other woman. "You were afraid you would continue the cycle."

"It just seemed smarter not to take any chances. And when Cam and I finally split, I knew the best thing I could ever do for Madeline was give custody to her father."

"You let him think you didn't want her."

"I didn't want her," Danica insisted.

But Ashley saw the pain in her eyes and she knew what it had cost Maddie's mother to give her up. She hadn't left her child because she didn't love her, but because she loved her too much to risk perpetuating the same kind of abuse she'd suffered. While the revelation didn't make Ashley like Danica any better, it did help her to understand the other woman. "Why are you telling me this?"

"Because I've finally realized that it's too late to undo the damage that I did to both Cam and Maddie, and I can see that you've helped both of them start healing."

Ashley wasn't entirely convinced of that, but Danica's words gave her hope that maybe she and Cam and Maddie could all do some healing together.

Chapter Fifteen

Thanksgiving dinner at Megan and Gage's was pure chaos, but in a good way. Having grown up with just one sister before Paige came to live with them, Ashley had never experienced a family meal that was quite so busy or loud or…fun.

She was immediately entranced by Gage's four nieces. Although the girls ranged in age from seven to twelve and had very different personalities, each one was charming in her own way. But Ashley enjoyed watching the interaction between Tess and Craig, too, observing the little touches and subtle signals that revealed a deep connection and enduring affection even after four kids. She saw evidence of the same bond between Megan and Gage and knew that her sister had truly lucked out when she'd fallen in love with Gage and married into the Richmond family.

Paige caught her in the kitchen, where she'd escaped on the pretext of wrapping up some of the leftover food but was really trying to fight the melancholic mood that had overtaken her.

"What's wrong?" her cousin asked, because she knew Ashley well enough to know that something was.

Ashley sighed. "I was just thinking about how lucky Megan is, to be with Gage, to be part of his family."

Paige opened her mouth as if there was something she intended to say, but closed it again without speaking a word.

"Come on, Paige. It's not like you to hold back if there's something on your mind."

"You don't want to hear it."

"I do," Megan said, coming into the kitchen with another armful of dishes.

"I just think that, instead of feeling sorry for herself, Ashley should go after what she wants."

"I'm not feeling sorry for myself," Ashley denied.

"Please—I can practically hear the violins."

"Paige," Megan admonished gently.

"I don't mean to be unsympathetic, but I had dinner last night with my friend Olivia—the one with the baby. She invited me over because she didn't want to celebrate the holiday alone but she has no family of her own, other than the baby, and she's had no contact with Emma's father since she told him she was pregnant. She didn't choose to be raising her child alone, but that's how it's working out.

"You made the decision to cut Cam out of your life, because I know that if it was up to him, he would be here with you right now. So if you're feeling neglected and alone, it's your own fault for not recognizing love when it's staring you right in the eye." And with that, she turned on her heel and stormed out of the kitchen.

"Well, that was quite a speech," Ashley said, as surprised as she was chastised by her cousin's outburst.

Megan slid an arm around hers sister's shoulder. "I think Olivia's really struggled with the adjustment from career woman to single mom, and it infuriates Paige that the father is doing nothing to help."

"Because it reminds her of her own father."

"Probably," her sister agreed.

"But she's right," Ashley realized. "And the truth is, I *don't* want to have this baby alone."

"I don't know why any woman in her right mind would," Megan said.

"But I'm scared," she admitted. "Cam and I have already screwed up our relationship twice. What if we try to make this work and screw it up again? Then we're not the only ones who get hurt—Maddie and her sister or brother will suffer, too."

"But what if you don't screw it up?"

And Ashley realized she'd been so focused on the potential negatives, she hadn't let herself fully consider the possibilities.

If she and Cam decided to work on their relationship and managed to succeed, then they could be a family. She would have everything she'd always wanted.

To say that Cameron was surprised when Ashley showed up at his door long after the turkey had been cleared away on Thanksgiving night would have been a colossal understatement. After their disastrous confrontation when he found out about her pregnancy, and his subsequent conversation with his father, he hadn't made any effort to see her or talk to her. He'd been clear about what he wanted, now it was up to Ashley to decide what she wanted.

As he put on a pot of decaf coffee, he wondered if her appearance at his door meant that she'd made a decision. But she didn't say anything until the coffee was made and he'd poured them each a cup.

"I thought Danica was in town."

Her mention of his ex-wife was another surprise, and definitely not a topic he wanted to discuss again.

"Yes, she is," he agreed.

"Is she here?"

"No, she's staying at a hotel downtown. We decided that would be a better arrangement from here on in."

"Oh."

"Did you come here to see me or her?"

"You," she said immediately. "And Maddie."

"She's in bed already."

Ashley nodded. "I didn't realize it was so late."

"It's not, really, but she had a busy day."

"Lots of turkey?"

"And too much pumpkin pie."

She nodded again, and he wondered if she felt half as awkward as he did. He wished he could go back a few months—even a few weeks—and change the way he'd handled things. Maybe then they'd still be together, looking forward to a future together.

"I've been thinking about what you said—the last time we talked," Ashley told him. "And I realized that I needed to clear up some of your misconceptions."

She wrapped her hands around the mug, stared into it. "When you found out I was pregnant, you accused me of only wanting a baby. But the truth is, after you came back to town, I never wanted *a* child so much as I wanted *your* child."

Her words, even more than the fact that she'd shown up at his door, gave him hope that maybe a future together wasn't completely out of reach, but he remained silent, cautious.

"And even if I hadn't gotten pregnant, I would have been happy. I *was* happy—with you and Maddie." She looked up at him now. "And I've been miserable without you."

"We've been pretty miserable, too," he admitted.

Those beautiful violet eyes filled with hope. "So…maybe… we could try again?"

It was what he wanted, what he hadn't dared let himself hope for when he saw her standing at his door, but as eager as he was to assure her, this time he wasn't agreeing to anything until he was sure they were on the same page.

"What is it, exactly, that you want to try?" he asked cautiously.

"I want us to be a family," she told him. "You and me and Maddie and our baby."

"Can I ask what precipitated this change of heart?" he asked, still cautious.

"I can't blame you for wondering, and I want to assure you that it doesn't have anything to do with the fact that I could lose my job, because—"

"What do you mean, you could lose your job?"

She flushed. "Oh. I thought you knew about that."

"About what?" He frowned.

"It doesn't matter," she said, opting not to mention his ex-wife's role in things. "My point is, deciding I wanted to be with you wasn't a change of heart at all. It just took me a while to acknowledge what was in my heart."

Which meant, if he was reading between the lines correctly, that she was—finally—admitting that she loved him.

"I would have told you about the baby," she continued. "I don't know how or when, but I never intended to keep my pregnancy a secret forever. I want my baby to know his or her father, and to know his or her big sister."

She pushed back her chair, stood up. "Anyway, that's what I wanted to tell you."

He stood up, too, and followed her down the hall. He didn't want to let her go, not with so much still unresolved between them. But he sensed that they both needed some time to assimilate everything before they moved forward, and he was determined to do better than an impulsive angry proposal the next time he asked Ashley to be his wife.

She paused at the door. "You once asked me if I believed in second chances."

He nodded. "I remember."

"Apparently I do believe in them after all."

"And third chances?" he prompted.

She smiled. "Maybe it's not the number of chances that matters as much as finally getting it right."

And as he watched her walk home, he was determined to ensure that this time they *would* get it right.

On Saturday, Maddie called Ashley to invite her to come over to for a movie marathon of *Shrek, Shrek Two* and *Shrek The Third*—her all-time favorite movies. Ashley wasn't sure what to make of the fact that the invitation had come from Cam's daughter instead of Cam, but she'd missed them both so much that she didn't hesitate.

They snuggled on the couch—Maddie tucked between her dad and Ashley—and ate popcorn and drank fruit punch. By the time the credits were rolling at the end of the second movie, Maddie was struggling to keep her eyes open.

"And now I think it's time for someone to brush her teeth and go to bed," Cam said, lifting his daughter up onto his shoulders and carting her toward the stairs.

"What about the third movie?"

"We can watch that one tomorrow," he promised her.

"And story time?" Maddie asked, not willing to relinquish that part of her bedtime routine despite her obvious fatigue.

"A short story," her dad agreed.

"Can Ashley tell me a story tonight?" Maddie turned to look beseechingly in Ashley's direction.

"Actually," Cam interrupted, "I had a story in mind for tonight."

Madeline frowned. "You only read stories from books."

"That's usually true," he admitted. "But I've been working on one that I thought you might like to hear."

"A made-up story? Is it any good?"

Cam's smile was wry. "I'll let you and Ashley be the judges of that."

So Ashley lowered herself onto the floor beside Maddie's bed while the little girl snuggled down under her covers.

"Once upon a time, in a land far, far away…"

Cam began his story in traditional fashion and proceeded to spin a fantastical tale about a beautiful princess who had fallen in love at a very young age with a handsome prince. And though the prince loved her, too, he had been given the gift of a magical sword and he wanted to travel the world and slay dragons, because he believed his desires and ambitions were far more important than a girl who had nothing to offer but all of the love in her heart.

"So the prince said goodbye to the princess and set out with his magic sword. And over the next twelve years, he slew more dragons than he'd ever imagined one man could slay, and he met many people and made many friends, but still there was an empty place in his heart. One of his friends was a very wise old man named Linus."

"Linus?" Maddie wrinkled her nose.

Cam scowled at the interruption. "What's wrong with Linus?"

"A fairy tale needs a fairy," she told him. "Preferably one with sparkly wings."

"Who's telling this story?"

"You are, Daddy, but—"

"One of those friends," he said again, "was a fairy named Linus—"

Maddie giggled.

"—who said to the prince, 'You have wealth and fame beyond your wildest dreams, but there is no love in your life.'"

"'That's not true,' the prince denied. 'I love Oscar, my loyal pet monkey, and I love all of my friends, and I especially love strawberry sundaes.'

"The sparkle-winged fairy shook his head. 'There is a different kind of love—the kind that a man feels for the woman who is his soul mate, the one who will stand by him and grow old with him—as he will stand by and grow old with her—until the stars fall from the sky. Have you never experienced this kind of love?'

"The prince was silent for a minute, remembering.

"'Once,' he finally said. 'A very long time ago.'

"'And did she love you?' Linus asked.

"'She said she did,' he recalled. 'But I thought she was too young to know what was in her heart, and I was too young to trust in my own.'

"'You are older now,' his friend pointed out.

"And so the prince strapped on his sword, tucked his monkey under his arm, and turned toward home. When he finally arrived back in the village, he was amazed to find that his feelings for the princess were even stronger now than they'd been so many years before.

"So the prince got down on one knee," Cam continued the story, but he was looking at Ashley while he spoke, and the intensity of his gaze stole all of the breath from her lungs. "And he took the princess's hand in his, vowed to love her forever and ever, and finally asked if she would do him the honor of becoming his bride."

"What did she say?" Madeline demanded when he fell silent again. "Did the princess agree to marry him?"

"What do you think?" Cam asked Ashley. "Would she accept his proposal?"

He wasn't asking about the fictional story, he was asking about their future. He was laying it all on the line right here in front of his daughter, showing that Maddie was part of the package that included his heart, his family, their future.

She had to swallow before she could speak, but then she assured him, "I think, if the prince really did love the princess enough to actually ask the question, she would most likely say yes."

"And then they would live happily-ever-after," Madeline announced.

"And then they would live happily-ever-after," her father agreed.

Maddie beamed. "That was a really good story."

"I'm glad you liked it," Cam told her.

"Will you tell me about Oscar tomorrow night?"

"Oscar?" He looked at her blankly.

"A pet monkey named Oscar should really have a story of his own."

"I'll have to think on that," Cam said, and kissed his daughter—first one cheek, then the other, then the tip of her nose.

Maddie giggled. "'Night, Daddy."

"Go straight to sleep now."

"Wait."

He paused.

"Can I have a drink of water? Please?"

"Didn't you have a drink before you got into bed?"

She nodded. "But I'm thirsty again."

"A quick drink," he reluctantly agreed. "Then no more stalling."

While Cam went to get her drink, Ashley pulled the covers up under Maddie's chin.

"Are you going to say yes?" Maddie whispered the question.

Ashley lowered herself onto the edge of the mattress. "Yes to what?" she asked cautiously.

The little girl rolled her eyes. "Didn't you pay any attention to his story?"

She couldn't help but smile at the indignant tone. "Yes, I paid attention to his story."

"Well, *he's* the prince," Maddie said, as if it was something Ashley should have figured out for herself. "And *you're* the princess. And if he loves you and you love him, then you should get married."

If only life was as simple as a fairy tale and happy endings were guaranteed, Ashley thought. But she'd learned long ago that there were no guarantees in life, and only more recently acknowledged that she was responsible for her own happiness.

And tonight she'd finally accepted that her greatest chance for happily-ever-after was with Cam, his little girl, their baby and the life they could build together.

"Would it be okay with you if we got married?"

Maddie's head bobbed enthusiastically. "Then you could be my new mommy."

"You have a mommy," Ashley felt compelled to remind her. Even if Danica had never been comfortable in that role, she was still the woman who had given birth to this amazing little girl and deserved to be acknowledged as her mother.

Maddie nodded again, with less enthusiasm this time. "But she's only a sometimes mommy, and I need an every day mommy like Victoria has."

"I kind of like the idea of being an every day mommy." She hugged the little girl, and though she knew she would have a baby of her own to cuddle in a few months, there was no doubt that Cam's firstborn would always hold a very special place in her heart.

When Cam came back into the room with a cup of water, Maddie took two tiny sips, then handed it back again.

"That's all you wanted?" he asked suspiciously.

She nodded.

He shook his head as he set the cup on the dresser. "Straight to sleep now."

She nodded again.

He turned out the light and led Ashley down the stairs and into the living room. Now that they were alone again, she worried that the awkwardness that had characterized their relationship of late might return, but then he took her in his arms, and she didn't feel awkward at all. She felt as if she was finally where she belonged.

"So," he said, pulling her into his arms. "What did you think of story time?"

She thought it was the most wonderful fairy tale she'd ever heard, but she wasn't quite ready to admit as much.

"Creative," she said. "But the magic sword? Talk about obviously and pathetically phallic."

"A dragon slayer needs a sword," he insisted, and tugged her down onto the couch beside him. "But if you think you could do better, you can help me with Oscar's adventures."

She shook her head. "His story line is entirely yours."

He shifted so that he was facing her, and stroked a finger gently down her cheek. "Actually, I was hoping we could work on it together. Maybe collaborate, over the next fifty or sixty years or more."

Her heart started pounding faster again. "That's a long-term collaboration," she warned.

"I figure it will take a while to get to the ever-after part."

"Is that your idea of a proposal?" she challenged.

"What do you think?"

As much as she wanted to throw her arms around him and

say yes a thousand times, she worried that giving in too soon would set a dangerous precedent for the next fifty or sixty years. She might finally be ready to admit that she loved him, but she didn't want to give him the impression that she was easy. Instead, she said, "I think you should stick to playing doctor."

He shifted closer, touched his lips lightly to hers. "Where did I screw up?"

"You skipped over the most important stuff," she told him.

He smiled. "You mean the stuff where I tell you how much I love you, have always loved you, and will always love you?"

"Yeah, that stuff."

"Okay," he said solemnly. "I love you Ashley Roarke, have always loved you and will always love you—until the stars fall from the sky."

"Ooh, that part about the stars…nice touch."

"Thanks." He took her hands, linked their fingers together. "Now would be a good time to tell me that you love me, too."

"I do love you," she admitted. "I always have and always will—until the stars fall from the sky."

He smiled. "So what do you say—will you marry me?"

"Will you slay dragons for me?" she asked him.

"Absolutely."

"Do I get to see the magic sword?"

"Honey, if you marry me, the magic sword is yours."

She leaned forward and touched her lips to his. "How could any girl refuse an offer like that?"

Epilogue

The night before Ashley and Cameron's wedding, an unexpected snowstorm blew through Pinehurst.

Being as it was the first Saturday in April, the bride had been prepared for rain—she hadn't anticipated snow. But even when she awoke to find the entire town buried beneath almost eight inches of fluffy white stuff, she wasn't concerned. She and Cameron had overcome much bigger obstacles to get to this point in their lives, and she knew that her husband-to-be wouldn't let anything get in the way of the ceremony, which was scheduled to take place later that morning.

Her mother wasn't quite so unruffled.

"It's April," Lillian Rolland fumed, stomping the snow off of her shoes inside the door. "There isn't supposed to be snow in April, and especially not on your wedding day."

Megan, who had managed to arrive even before the snowplows had been down the street, rolled her eyes behind their mother's back.

"You can't schedule the weather," Paige, who had driven in from Syracuse the day before, said philosophically.

"But I arranged for a horse-drawn carriage to take the bridal party to the church," Lillian reminded them.

She may have only had a few months to plan the wedding, but she hadn't overlooked any details. Since Megan had tied the knot with little notice and even less preparation at City Hall, Lillian had been determined to ensure that at least one of her daughters had a proper wedding, and she'd dragged her new husband away from their home in Europe and thrown herself into the preparations.

"If we can't have four horses, at least we have four-wheel drive," Ashley told her mother now.

"But I wanted to ride with the horses," Maddie chimed in.

Lillian brushed a hand affectionately over the child's hair. "At least someone here appreciates the details."

"Come on, Maddie," Paige steered the little girl toward the stairs and away from the battle she sensed was brewing. "Let's get you dressed."

"I appreciate everything you've done," Ashley assured her mother. "And I know that, because of all your careful planning, my wedding day is going to be wonderful. I just don't think anything—not my dress or flowers and especially not the weather—matters as much as finally marrying the man I love."

Her mother sighed. "You're right. Of course, you're right. I just wanted everything to be perfect for you."

"Everything will be," Ashley said, because she knew that being with Cam would make it true.

An hour and a half later, two horse-drawn sleighs glided to a halt in front of the Holy Trinity Church.

"It was just like riding in a fairy tale!" Maddie exclaimed.

"Personally, I would have much preferred a heated limo," Paige confided to Megan, as they followed the skipping child up the wide stone steps—which had been carefully shoveled clean and salted—toward the front doors.

Her cousin pulled her shawl more tightly around her shoulders. "Well, if we had to freeze our butts off, at least we did so in style."

As Ashley lifted her skirt to follow the others, she could barely feel her toes inside her satin pumps, but she didn't complain. Not just because she didn't want to offend her mother after she'd gone to such efforts to amend the transportation arrangements, but because she knew that Cam was waiting for her inside the church and that knowledge was enough to warm everything inside of her.

When the music began, Paige gave Ashley a quick hug— careful not to crush her flowers—before she started up the aisle. Megan went next, whispering, "Be happy," with a smile that assured her sister she knew she would be before she followed her cousin's path. Then it was Maddie's turn, and several guests would later remark that the little girl's smile was almost as radiant as the bride's.

For Maddie, this was the happiest day of her life, though she couldn't decide if it was because it was her daddy and Ashley's wedding day, or because she was getting a baby sister (she refused to consider that the baby might be a boy), or because she was going to Florida with Grandma and Grandpa for her spring break while the newlyweds went on their honeymoon.

It was the happiest day of Ashley's life, too, but she knew exactly why. Because she was finally married to the man she'd always loved. Because Cam and Maddie were now part of the family she'd always wanted.

And because her happily-ever-after was just beginning.

* * * * *

Look for Paige's story THE BABY SURPRISE
the next book in Brenda Harlen's new
Special Edition miniseries BRIDES & BABIES
On sale July 2010,
available wherever Silhouette Books are sold.

Harlequin Intrigue top author Delores Fossen presents
a brand-new series of breathtaking romantic suspense!
TEXAS MATERNITY: HOSTAGES
The first installment available May 2010:
THE BABY'S GUARDIAN

Shaw cursed and hooked his arm around Sabrina.

Despite the urgency that the deadly gunfire created, he tried to be careful with her, and he took the brunt of the fall when he pulled her to the ground. His shoulder hit hard, but he held on tight to his gun so that it wouldn't be jarred from his hand.

Shaw didn't stop there. He crawled over Sabrina, sheltering her pregnant belly with his body, and he came up ready to return fire.

This was obviously a situation he'd wanted to avoid at all cost. He didn't want his baby in the middle of a fight with these armed fugitives, but when they fired that shot, they'd left him no choice. Now, the trick was to get Sabrina safely out of there.

"Get down," someone on the SWAT team yelled from the roof of the adjacent building.

Shaw did. He dropped lower, covering Sabrina as best he could.

There was another shot, but this one came from a rifleman on the SWAT team. Shaw didn't look up, but he heard the sound of glass being blown apart.

The shots continued, all coming from his men, which meant it might be time to try to get Sabrina to better cover. Shaw glanced at the front of the building.

So that Sabrina's pregnant belly wouldn't be smashed against the ground, Shaw eased off her and moved her to a sitting position so that her back was against the brick wall. They were close. Too close. And face-to-face.

He found himself staring right into those sea-green eyes.

How will Shaw get Sabrina out?
Follow the daring rescue and the heartbreaking
aftermath in THE BABY'S GUARDIAN by Delores Fossen,
available May 2010 from Harlequin Intrigue.

HARLEQUIN
Ambassadors

Want to share your passion for reading Harlequin® Books?

Become a Harlequin Ambassador!

Harlequin Ambassadors are a group of passionate and well-connected readers who are willing to share their joy of reading Harlequin® books with family and friends.

You'll be sent all the tools you need to spark great conversation, including free books!

All we ask is that you share the romance with your friends and family!

You'll also be invited to have a say in new book ideas and exchange opinions with women just like you!

To see if you qualify* to be a Harlequin Ambassador, please visit **www.HarlequinAmbassadors.com.**

*Please note that not everyone who applies to be a Harlequin Ambassador will qualify. For more information please visit www.HarlequinAmbassadors.com.

Thank you for your participation.

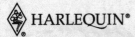

LAURA MARIE ALTOM

The Baby Twins

Stephanie Olmstead has her hands full raising
her twin baby girls on her own. When she runs
into old friend Brady Flynn, she's shocked to find
herself suddenly attracted to the handsome airline
pilot! Will this flyboy be the perfect daddy—
or will he crash and burn?

Babies
&
Bachelors
USA

"LOVE, HOME & HAPPINESS"

www.eHarlequin.com

HAR75309

Love Inspired

Former bad boy Sloan Hawkins is back in
Redemption, Oklahoma, to help keep his aunt's
cherished garden thriving and to reconnect with the
girl he left behind, Annie Markham. But when he
discovers his secret child—and that single mother
Annie never stopped loving him—he's determined
that a wedding will take place in the garden
nurtured by faith and love.

REDEMPTION RIVER

Where healing flows...

Look for

The Wedding Garden
by Linda Goodnight

*Available May 2010
wherever you buy books.*

Steeple
Hill®

www.SteepleHill.com

REQUEST YOUR FREE BOOKS!

2 FREE NOVELS PLUS 2 FREE GIFTS!

SPECIAL EDITION

Life, Love and Family!

YES! Please send me 2 FREE Silhouette® Special Edition® novels and my 2 FREE gifts (gifts are worth about $10). After receiving them, if I don't wish to receive any more books, I can return the shipping statement marked "cancel." If I don't cancel, I will receive 6 brand-new novels every month and be billed just $4.24 per book in the U.S. or $4.99 per book in Canada. That's a saving of 15% off the cover price! It's quite a bargain! Shipping and handling is just 50¢ per book.* I understand that accepting the 2 free books and gifts places me under no obligation to buy anything. I can always return a shipment and cancel at any time. Even if I never buy another book from Silhouette, the two free books and gifts are mine to keep forever.

235/335 SDN E5RG

Name	(PLEASE PRINT)	
Address		Apt. #
City	State/Prov.	Zip/Postal Code

Signature (if under 18, a parent or guardian must sign)

Mail to the **Silhouette Reader Service:**
IN U.S.A.: P.O. Box 1867, Buffalo, NY 14240-1867
IN CANADA: P.O. Box 609, Fort Erie, Ontario L2A 5X3

Not valid for current subscribers to Silhouette Special Edition books.

Want to try two free books from another line?
Call 1-800-873-8635 or visit www.morefreebooks.com.

* Terms and prices subject to change without notice. Prices do not include applicable taxes. N.Y. residents add applicable sales tax. Canadian residents will be charged applicable provincial taxes and GST. Offer not valid in Quebec. This offer is limited to one order per household. All orders subject to approval. Credit or debit balances in a customer's account(s) may be offset by any other outstanding balance owed by or to the customer. Please allow 4 to 6 weeks for delivery. Offer available while quantities last.

Your Privacy: Silhouette is committed to protecting your privacy. Our Privacy Policy is available online at www.eHarlequin.com or upon request from the Reader Service. From time to time we make our lists of customers available to reputable third parties who may have a product or service of interest to you. If you would prefer we not share your name and address, please check here. ☐

Help us get it right—We strive for accurate, respectful and relevant communications. To clarify or modify your communication preferences, visit us at www.ReaderService.com/consumerschoice.

SSE10R